Vision of Change

*Sequel of 'Til Death Do Us Part:
A Marriage Survives the Stress of Military Life*

Viranda I. Slappy

Copyright © 2018 by Viranda I. Slappy

Printed in the United States of America

ISBN: Paperback: 978-1-948172-07-3
          Hardback: 978-1-948172-16-5
          eBook: 978-1-948172-08-0

Library of Congress Control Number: 2018935660

STONEWALL PRESS
PAVING YOUR WAY TO SUCCESS

Stonewall Press
363 Paladium Court
Owings Mills, MD 21117
www.stonewallpress.com
1-888-334-0980

Author Website Information:

www.booksandauthors.net/Interviews/VISlappy.html
www.mdw.army.mil/news/Til_Death_Do_Us_Part.html
www.geocities.com/slappyviranda/authorvirandaslappy
www.wxbh.com/express_yourself.htm
www.wxbh.com/express_yourself_schedule.htm

It is an honor for me to dedicate this novel to my
mother-in-law, Mary Mitchell-Slappy, and my
devoted husband, John Cecil Slappy Senior

CONTENTS

ACKNOWLEDGMENTS

First, I want to give my recognition to God for bestowing me with the greatest gift to create this story.

I extend special thanks to all the people who shared their life experience to make it possible for this reality-based book to be available for all to read.

Special thanks to Corliss Barner for her supportive idealism character and friendship.

To my husband and children, thanks for your loving support and encouragement to continue the sequel Vision of Change.

Special thanks to Zsashamica D. Slappy, my editor, daughter, and friend for your devotional patience, knowledge, skills, and ability to produce this book.

To my book Photography, special thanks to McTavish Photography & Video, Junction City, Kansas for author photo.

To my book artist, thanks for your artistic talents in creating my book cover.

I want to extend special thanks to my readers for your continuous inspirational support, devotional time and enthusiasm for the purchase of all my books.

INTRODUCTION

The story you are about to read is the sequel of *Til Death Do Us Part: A Marriage Survives the Stress of Military Life* is based on the true experiences of military spouses throughout the armed forces network. You will discover the continuous encounters of a military couple, Virginia and Carlos Slaughter, new beginnings as they capture their challenging destiny in order to make their dreams come true.

CHAPTER ONE

JOURNEY TO THE UNITED STATES

After the tour in Berlin was over, the Slaughters received orders for an assignment in Fort Jackson, South Carolina in December 1991. The family was excited about returning to the United States, but they also have fears. The family prepared for their adventurous assignment, wondering what it would be like to live among a society that they weren't a part of for five years. Their children often spoke of their fear of gangs and reuniting with family who they didn't see in a long time. The children were in elementary when they left the states, and now they are teen age and preteen age level. Carlene was a junior in high school and Carlos Jr was in middle school. The children often spoke about their fears dealing with peers and gangs, but Virginia and Carlos assured them that they will learn how to adapt to their fear of change.

The family boarded a 747 Lufthansa flight to Frankfurt with a connecting flight to John F. Kennedy Airport, then New York to their final destination, Atlanta, Georgia. The family will leave behind the memories of friends, impact of Desert Storm, and falling of the Iron Curtain to a new beginning of change. Their flight to the United States was approximately eight hours. On the plane, Carlene and Junior were very excited because they were returning home as a family again. Carlene was very observant of her mother's behavior. Virginia appeared to be a thousand miles away.

"Mom, are you alright?"

"Yes, honey. Why are you asking?"

"Well, Mom, to me you seem be a thousand miles away. I bet I know what is on your mind. You can't wait to see grandma, huh? And you're worried about how they are going to react to dad and his drinking problem, how it caused him to hurt you. Mom, everything is going to be alright. You'll see.

"How did you know what's on my mind?"

"I'm your daughter, aren't I? I will always know what you're thinking." Carlene embraced her mother.

"Are you alright, Virginia?" Carlos asked.

"I'm fine. Carlene and I were just sharing our thoughts on how we can't wait to be among family again.

"Me, too," Carlos and Junior said simultaneously.

"Alright, enough about home. Let's enjoy our last flight and German food, 'cause we won't be getting this anymore."

"Amen!" Carlos and Junior said simultaneously.

"You all are crazy," Virginia said.

"Yep, and we got that from you and dad," Junior said.

The flight landed in JFK. Carlos told the family to fasten their seatbelts. They were excited looking out of the window as the plane proceeds landed. The Slaughters exited the plane and Carlos yelled pulled junior to his side.

"We have no idea what this area is like, so don't go wondering off, do you her me, Junior?

"Yes, Dad! Why do you always pick on me when we go places?"

"Because you are the one who will wonder off. Right Carlene?

"Right, Dad!" Carlene said.

The family looked for the gate connects their flight to Atlanta. Pushing through the crowd as they boarded the subway shuttle taking them to their gate terminal, they boarded Delta Airlines.

"Dad, did you tell grandma when we are coming?"

"Junior, you know dad didn't tell grandma. Dad likes surprising his mama, but I bet mom told her," Carlene said.

"Yep, I sure did. But I didn't tell her what time we would be there."

"Boy, I can't wait to see my cousins, Kirk and Kesha. I wonder how big they have gotten," Junior said.

"I bet Kirk is big and, of course, Kesha might be as well," Virginia said.

"Mom, I know that Kirk has gotten big cause he loves to eat, but I doubt if Kesha's gotten any taller," Carlene said.

The pilot announced the flight is landing. The family looked out of window again, excited as they are finally home. Carlos yelled about the seatbelts again.

"Mom, why dad always yellin' 'fasten your seatbelt'?"

"Now, you know your dad. he hates to fly and is just trying to ensure our protection. After all, he's your Father, and what did I tell you of the responsibilities of a father?"

"I know, he's the head of the household and protects us. But, Mom, does he have to tell us that every time?"

"Yep, he will do whatever it takes to ensure our safety.

After all, who's in charge?"

"Dad is, but he treats us like we are his soldiers."

"Alright, Junior, where are you supposed to be?"

"I know, Dad, by your side and not wonder off."

The Slaughters exit the plane and were happy to know that they are just one and a half hours from home. The family pushed through a crowd again, heading for the connecting terminal to retrieve their baggage.

"Carlos, did you get a rental car?"

"Yeah, we got to pick up our luggage and then we are going to get a car."

They gathered their luggage and rushed to the Rental ar section. They loaded their car with their luggage and began their trip home in Macon, Georgia. While traveling down I-75 highway, Junior was anxious to see Kirk and Kesha.

"Dad, how long will it take to drive to Macon, Georgia?"

"Well, Son, it should take at least one hour and thirty minutes."

"Wow, Dad, that's a long time! Did you tell grandma when we are coming?"

"No, I told you I want to surprise them."

"Will y'all be quiet, I'm trying to sleep. Junior, you better get you some sleep 'cause you know when we get to grandma's house, everybody is going to be there, and we won't go to bed until about three o'clock in the morning."

"Your Mom is snoring," Carlos said, placing his hands-on Virginia's face. He drove on and saw the sign saying Forsyth, Georgia. He knew that he's only thirty minutes away from home. He glanced at Virginia and the kids, thanking God for a safe trip returning with his family.

"Y'all need to wake up! We almost here! Carlene, Mom, wake up! We almost at grandma's house!"

"Oh, we are at mama's house!" Virginia said.

Carlos drove the car in the driveway. Mrs. Cottingham and Virginia's siblings all came rushing out the house when they saw the car at the driveway. Virginia and her family emerged from the vehicle, all smiling happy to be home. Mrs. Cottingham smiled, reaching out to embrace her daughter, whispering she's is so glad she made it home. Hugging and kissing her mother, Virginia said, "Mama, I'm home!"

Coming out last, Carlos observed the joy in their eyes. Mrs. Cottingham walked towards him and gave him a hug, whispering welcome home.

"Yeah, I'm glad to be home with my family," Carlos said.

Virginia sat on the couch and stared at the family laughing and talking with love and joy. Virginia's sister Tricia and niece Shawn sat next to her.

"What's up, Aunt Virginia?" Shawn asked. "You mighty quiet!"

"Your aunt is very tired. We had a long trip!" Virginia said.

"Well, one thing I say about aunt Virginia: You still is looking good. I told mama not to worry because I knew you were not going to let yourself go! See, Mom? Aunt Virginia still wearing her makeup!"

"Now, Tricia knows I'll always wear my makeup. I been wearing makeup sense I was in high school, so what makes you think I'm going to stop now?"

"Well, when you and uncle Carlos call saying that y'all was having marital problems, the first thing mom and grandma thought you had gain a lot of weight and let yourself go. I told them that you hadn't and that I'm going to be just like Aunt Virginia."

"Yeah, she did say that! Shawn is mess, Gina!" Tricia said.

"I see, and she definitely is not that little girl I left years ago. Come here and give a big hug. So, I know we are going to be hanging tight while I'm home."

"You know it. I already told mom that I will be spending all my time with you while she at work," Shawn said.

"Okay. Let's get ready to go and see your other grandma. Junior, go and get your mama's and Carlene's luggage out of the car so we won't have to do that when we bring them back," Carlos said.

"I know y'all got to go visit Carlos mother." Mrs. Cottingham rose up from her chair and reached for Virginia and her grandchildren. "Yep, we'll be back. You know she wants to see everyone too. Mama,

Carlene, and I will be staying with you and Carlos and Junior will be staying at Mrs. Slaughter's house," Virginia said.

"I'll be waiting up for you all." Mrs. Cottingham escorted Virginia and the kids to door.

"Okay, Mom." Virginia hugged her mother.

The Slaughters head for grandma Slaughter's. As they drove up into the driveway, there was no one waiting for them. Carlos didn't say when he was arriving. They all went to the door. He rang the doorbell and grandma Slaughter came to the door.

Mrs. Slaughter Screamed. "Oh my God! It's Carlos and his family!" She told her sister on the phone. "It's Carlos, Hazel, I'll call you back!" She reached for Carlos, laughing while she hugged him, then hugged Virginia and the kids as they all walked in. "When did y'all get here?"

"We've been here for a while now. We stopped by Virginia's family's house first," Carlos said.

"Come here, Junior; let me see how you look. Boy, you sure have grown."

"Yep, I'm not that little boy anymore. I'm all grown up!"

"Carlene, stand up and let me look at you. My you're not wearing chubby clothes now. You have lost weight. Virginia, I thought you were at least weighting 200lbs."

"Why is everybody thinking that? I gain weight, but I'm wearing 9 and 10 women's clothing size."

"No, you still are looking good!"

"Mom, don't go telling her that!"

"No, you all are looking good! Let me call and let the rest of the family know you all are home."

The rest of family came over to her house to greet Carlos and his family. It was getting late, so Carlos had to take Virginia and Carlene over to Mrs. Cottingham's because where will be staying, and Virginia can spend time with her family and he and junior will visit every day.

Meanwhile at the Cottinghams', Mrs. Cottingham was wrapping up a conversation with her sister on how well her Virginia and her family are looking. Tricia and Shawn sat in the family room, waiting for Virginia and Carlene to return, they discussed how Virginia appeared to be happy, and whatever issues the Slaughter family had dealt with while in Berlin, they survived and return home. This might be the first time with this type of issue that's derived among family members and yet reunited. This was a turning point for everyone. They could not wait to hear how they survived that turmoil. Minutes later, a knock was at the door. It was Carlos dropping off Virginia and Carlene. They unpacked their luggage, showered, and changed for bed. Mrs. Cottingham was in bed, waiting for Virginia to come and have a mother and daughter talk. But little did she know that all her girls were joining Virginia and Carlene to listen to their experiences in Berlin.

Virginia and Carlene shared many stories to them that night about their adventures. The most interesting one they wanted to know was how Virginia's and Carlos's marriage survived Carlos's addiction to alcohol, and what caused the domestic violence that lead to Virginia's physical injuries. Virginia explained that Carlos was a victim of alcohol; none of them knew that this was the cause of many of their marriage disputes. But through time, and Virginia's determination, they discovered through their local resources that Carlos had symptoms of an alcoholic.

Virginia revealed her intense therapy with her favorite counselor, Renata, who was an admirer of her courage. Virginia's courage directed her to discover her weakness and contribution to an illness neither of them were aware of. How Virginia's independence enabling Carlos's drinking. She was a woman who wanted the best that life and ensured that her family was a recipient of those qualities. Therefore, she ensured that the household was taken cared of, in all aspects. But this only gave Carlos time to increase his drinking that lead to alcoholism. Virginia had no idea that Carlos was a victim of alcohol during his teenage years, even when they were childhood lovers who eventually married. Their lack of knowledge of alcoholism is the reason why the family suffers for so many years. Her love for Carlos gave her the courage to end the crisis, but almost caused her her life due to the approach selected to resolve it.

Virginia explained to her mother that she was directed not to confront Carlos for fear of his reactions, but she didn't think that he would ever hurt her, not realizing that an alcoholic cannot be trusted while intoxicated. So, that night, Virginia confronted him about her intentions to getting help, and Carlos lost control, which caused a fight. Virginia explained how hurt and shocked she was when the incident occurred. She mentioned how the children could not believe the violence Carlos had displayed, as if he had become a different person. He was determined not to go to counseling neither was her. But Virginia recovered, and Carlos was admitted to the rehabilitation facility, which lead to a new beginning for the family.

Mrs. Cottingham was angry once she heard the news and just wanted her child and grandchildren to return home. But now that she saw Virginia and her family, she realized her daughter made a courageous decision that was worthwhile.

During the weeks Virginia and her family spent visiting, they began to heal. The animosity that the families had for both Virginia and Carlos began to fade. Their families saw how Virginia, Carlos, and children were communicating as a family, and the change they all encounter for the better without the abuse of alcohol. Mrs. Cottingham acknowledged how she noticed Carlos's undying love for Virginia and the children. She was pleased and had peace in her heart again for her son-in-law, who she once hated. Though she said that it was not him she hated, but his behavior that drove him to lose control and hurt her daughter. She dealt with his feelings differently. He confronted him once he returned and expressed her anger. She said she never wants this to happen again or he will answer to her.

Weeks passed and Carlos constantly made telephone calls to department of army assignment to get his orders changed to Fort Stewart located in Savannah, Georgia. Within that same week, Carlos drove to Fort Jackson, South Carolina, to pick his car up that was shipped from Berlin. Weeks after observing the growth of the family and community, this inspired the Slaughters to be part of this change. So, Carlos prioritized his reassignment. His determinations got a response from the Personnel Reassignment Section, providing diversion orders to Carlos, attaching him to Fort Stewart. The news brought joy to the families. Finally, they will get the opportunity to be part of their children's and grandchildren's growth. Carlos, Virginia, and children prepared for travel.

Fort Stewart and Hunter Army Airfield are the home of the "Mechanized" 3rd Infantry Division and combined to be the army's premier power projection platform on the Atlantic Coast. It is the largest, most effective and efficient armor training base east of the Mississippi, covering 280,000 acres including parts of Liberty, Long, Tattnall, Evans and Bryan counties in southeast Georgia. Hunter Army Airfield is home to the army's longest runway on the east coast (11,375 feet) and the Truscott Air Deployment Terminal. Together, these assets are capable of deploying units such as the heavy armored forces of the 3rd Infantry Division or the elite light fighters of the 1st Battalion, 75th Ranger Regiment.

Carlos and the family left in January 1991 heading for Fort Stewart, informing the family that they will be home for the weekend.

Carlos and his family arrived at Fort Stewart. They stayed at the post guest house facility. Carlos and Virginia got their kids into the school system. One evening, the kids returned from school saying how they missed the friends they left behind in Germany. They told of how school was different in the States, with gangs visible. Virginia and Carlos discussed the importance of not to get drawn into participating and never fear sharing how they feel or needs for guidance when facing peer pressure, whether its sex or drugs.

Carlos changed the subject and brought brochures of realtors in the area. The family reviewed them and Virginia and the kids were excited about their new beginnings and adventures finally owning their own home. Carlos told Virginia that they will be going house hunting. Of course, the kids wanted to be a part of this adventure, but they cannot miss school, so it will be just Virginia and Carlos. But they kept in mind the children's input on their own space and privacy. Carlos and Virginia went and met with realtors, going on many house hunting interviews. They finally found a house they both agreed to purchase. The house had an outdoor pool area for the kids and plenty of yard space for Junior to play basketball. Those were the special additions the kids loved when Carlos and Virginia presented the features of the house.

The weekend came and the Slaughters packed and headed home to Macon to share their news about their new home. Everyone was glad for the Slaughters, especially Mrs. Cottingham. Finally, her daughter will be in driving distance, and, of course, the joy of Mrs. Slaughter that her son will be near. It was as if God had brought joy to the entire family. The kids said that they liked school, even though things were a lot different from the military communities. They weren't free to travel on bus or train or going shopping, attending youth center activities, hanging out with their friends. Instead, their lifestyle changed from living among military families to living among a diverse community with fear of turmoil; pressure of sex, drugs and gangs. The family was aware of the challenges and prepared to face these challenges as a family reunited forever. Carlos and Virginia spent the weekend with family, laughing among relatives. This was the first time the Slaughters spent the Christmas holidays with family, exchanging gifts and enjoying their favorite "soul food" dishes. The time came for them to part, but their departure was pleasant because everyone knew were only a few miles and they will be seeing them again.

Carlos reported to work and his commander requested him to his office. He was notified that Carlos's order had been rescind and reassigned to Fort Riley, Kansas. This news broke Carlos's heart. Finally, he brought good news to his family being among their relatives but now the army decided to reassign him to Kansas. He explained to the commander that he was in the process of purchasing a house and the kids enrolled in school, and now the army wants him to pack up and take them to Kansas. The commander looked at Carlos, saying how sorry he was this did not work in his favor, and how he hated that he will be losing an outstanding soldier, but those are the cards they're dealt with when joining the armed forces: mission first and family last. He ensured him that his family will understand and support his new assignment.

Carlos left the commander's office disappointed, hating to be the one to bring bad news. Carlos arrived at the hotel returning early from work. Virginia knew that something was wrong and thought it had to do with the house. Carlos sat on the bed and told Virginia he was reassigned to Fort Riley. Virginia was disappointed and could not understand how they could do this. Interviewing Slaughter about his family, and did it matter that they had placed their children in school and bought a home? Carlos said it doesn't matter and thanked God they found out before they closed on the house. The question was, will Virginia and the kids accept his new assignment and join him at Kansas? Looking dismayed, Virginia smiled and said, "What's our reporting date?"

Carlos grabbed Virginia, looking into her big eyes, telling her how much he loved her and that he knew how much she wanted to be near her family, but assured her they will visit often. "Well, Dear, now we got to tell the kids that we are headed to the Land of OZ. Fort Riley, Kansas, here we come!"

The kids arrived from school wanting to know what was up with the new house and how they are moving into their new home. When Carlos and Virginia told the kids to settle down, they presented them with bad news. Carlene and Junior were disappointed about them not going to have the dream house with an outdoor pool. "But at least we have each other and our family will be together." Once again, the kids had to say farewell to their classmates and friends. The kids gathered their things up and asked about Carlos's new assignment. Carlene asked Virginia how she feels about her dad's new assignment. Virginia shared how much she is going to miss her family, especially her mother who has gotten older and how she missed out on so much of her mother's life. But she has her own family now and must support Carlos's career and assured Carlene that everything will be alright.

"God don't make no mistakes. If this is our new journey, he will see us through." She embraced Carlene.

"Mom, Grandma will be alright, you will see."

"I know, now go and get your things together, so we get ready to visit family before heading to Kansas."

The Slaughters processed out of Fort Stewart and headed home to visit family in Macon prior to their final designation, "the Big Red One". The Slaughters shared their news of Carlos's new assignment. The news brought sadness in the heart of their relatives who were looking forward to being part of the growth of their children and grandchildren. But Carlos's career embarked on a new adventure, meaning that they must share in their growth from a distance, promising they will return to visit often. Virginia confronted her mother with the news, and she gave her blessings, wishing her success. Virginia assured her mother once she had settled, she will return, hoping that she and the rest of the family will visit them. Mrs. Cottingham did not make any promises about her coming to Kansas but will be looking forward to her daughter's visit and was glad that they are in calling distance. The Cottinghams and Slaughters gathered among family with Mrs. Slaughter's garnishing "Soul Food", enjoying and laughing among family and friends, expressing joy for Carlos's new assignment and new beginning.

The time had come for Carlos and Virginia to gather up their belongings and say their good-byes to their family. Virginia and Carlene were staying with her mother. Carlos called Virginia to let her know when he will be arriving to pick her up. It was a very long drive, approximately eighteen hours. Virginia hated good-byes, especially leaving her mother and grandmother, but her grandmother knew that she will be alright.

"You know, Gina, you and your aunt are the only one who have left Macon and survived on your own. Now, I'm not going to worry, nor will your mother, because we know you are going to be well. So, go with your husband and enjoy. Include God in your life, you and your family will survive because that's where you belong, remember God makes no mistake. As long as you proved that see how the Lord has brought you through and return you home united with your husband and family. Girl, go and keep God among your midst and you will rise to the highest level of success, because your grandma will be praying for you and your family. go and be happy with Slaughter. He's a good man and I thank God that you found him… give me a hug and go!"

"Okay, Grandma! I'm going and keep praying." Virginia wiped her tears.

"Well, Sis, I sure hate you all are leaving us going to Kansas, but God knows best!" Tricia said.

"Yes, he does, Sis, so Kansas here we come." Virginia embraced her sister. "Now, you take good care of our mama."

"You know, I will. Don't be surprised when I call and say I'm on my way out there."

"I won't be surprised as long as you bring mom!"

"Now, you know it's going to be hard to get mom to come out there. I'm probably going to fly, so you know if mom is going to come. You and Slaughter are going to have to come and pick mom up. That's the only way she will travel."

"Well, Mom, when you want to come to Kansas, you know all you have to do is let me know and I will come pick you up."

Tears were in Mrs. Cottingham's eyes. "I know you will!"

"Mom, why are you crying?"

"Well, I guess the time has come again for me to say good-bye and you know I hate doing that, and I wish that you did not have to go… but your place is with your husband and like your grandma said, he is a good man."

The phone rang, and it was Mr. Cottingham calling to speak with Virginia before she left.

"Are you all going to come by for a visit?" Mr. Cottingham said.

"Yes, Dad, as soon as Carlos comes, we all will come by the house." Virginia hung up the phone."

"What did he say?" Mrs. Cottingham said.

"Mom, dad just wanted to know if we are going to stop by his house. I really don't feel like putting up with my stepmother, Helen. But you know I got to go and spend time with him."

"I know your dad loves you too. Make sure you all call me before you leave your dad, because I know you will be getting on the highway driving to Kansas departing from his house."

"Mom, I will make sure I call you."

"Carlene, let me get my hug from you and when your dad and Junior arrive, I will get my hug from Junior. Grandma hates to see y'all go, but I know you all want to be with your daddy."

"Yep, that we do!"

Carlos and Junior, rang the doorbell and came to pick up Virginia and Carlene. They said their good-byes. Carlos ensured Mrs.

Cottingham he will take good care of Virginia and his kids, saying that she needs to visit when they get settled in Kansas. "Junior, did you get your mom's and Carlene's luggage?"

"Yep, Dad, I got it and put them in the trunk."

"Mrs. Cottingham, I will be back. Let me check and make sure their luggage's are in the trunk of car alright."

"Grandma, I got to go and help dad load the trunk."

"Y'all go ahead. Carlene and Virginia will be in here. Junior sure has grown up. Gina, you sure have a great family. Mom is really proud of you. Y'all keep it up."

"Mom, I will! Sometime it's hard, because I'm not around you all, but as you all say, God knows best.'"

The Slaughters left Mrs. Cottingham's home and got in their car heading for Grandpa Cottingham. When they arrived at his house, Helen was out in the yard directing Carlos to drive around back to park. The Slaughters got out of the car and went to the backyard where Grandpa Cottingham was barbequing some ribs. Grandpa Cottingham was glad to see his son-in-law and embraced him.

"Boy! Carlos, I'm sure glad you all stop by before you left. Man, I thought you all were going to be stationed close to home." He kissed and hugged Virginia. "Gina, you sure do look good!"

"Dad, I'm trying to hang!"

"Dad is proud of you, too! Now let me see how Carlene and Junior are doing. Y'all are looking good, too."

"Grandpa, what that's you Barbequing? Hmm… it sure smells good!" Junior said.

"Y'all can go inside and fix y'all a plate. Y'all also can fix plate to take on the road. I know y'all will be hungry. That's why I told Helen that I was going to cook out today, because I want y'all to have some food to take with you on the road. Go in the house, I'm coming behind. Get something to eat."

Carlos and his family went in, sitting around family and friends enjoying barbeque.

"Cottingham, you sure know how to barbeque! I need to get your recipe so mine can turn out like yours," Carlos said.

Helen writes down the recipe and gives it to Carlos.

"Carlos, Helen and I will definitely plan a trip to visit y'all once I get my finances straight! Helen needs to stop doing all that shopping, plus we went to Florida and visited some of our friends, but once we get our finances straight, I plan to visit y'all."

"Come on out there!" Carlos said.

"Well, do you know how long you will be station there?"

"I'm hoping I can stay until I retire. I'm eligible to retire in five years. I know I will be there at least two; after that, I'm going to with DA and see if I can get close to home, because I'm ready to get out! Man, you get tired of moving your family from place to place. It starts to get old and that's how I'm feeling, but God knows best so I'm got to hang in there, because I got over ten years. It's going on fourteen years, so it's time for me to start settling down. I'm not getting any younger, my kids are getting older, Carlene will be graduating from high school soon, and I got to do something."

"Yell, I know what you mean. You definite need to be focusing on retiring, because before you know it, the kids are grown and on their own.

The Slaughter's continue to mingle among family and friends until time came for them to get on the road. Carlene reminded Virginia to call her grandma before leaving Grandpa's house to let her know what time they will be on the road heading for Kansas. Mr. Cottingham and Helen hugged and kissed Virginia and her family, wishing them the best and to be safe on the highway. Mr. Cottingham went around the car to Carlos's window.

"Carlos drive safe and I know you will take care of my daughter and grands. Don't forget to call once y'all arrive in Kansas."

Oh! Cottingham, you don't have to worry that's my sweet thing and I'm going to take care of Virginia because I don't know if I would be doing this; if it wasn't for Virginia's support. Man, we will call when we get there!"

As Carlos drove off, Carlene and Junior waved good-bye. "I love you, Grandpa!"

The Slaughters waved as they departed Mr. Cottingham's home, heading for I-70 highway to Fort Riley.

The Cantigny First Division Foundation was established in 1957 with the principal mission of promoting the history of the Big Red One, the famed 1st Infantry Division of the U.S. Army. As part of this mission, the foundation operates the First Division Museum at Cantigny and the Colonel Robert R. McCormick Research Center. It also publishes books, videos, and other materials on the history of the division. As a non-profit corporation, the foundation receives no federal, state, or local funds. Support from the Robert R. McCormick Tribune Foundation helps to make its many activities possible.

CHAPTER TWO

JOURNEY TO FORT RILEY KANSAS; THE BIG RED ONE

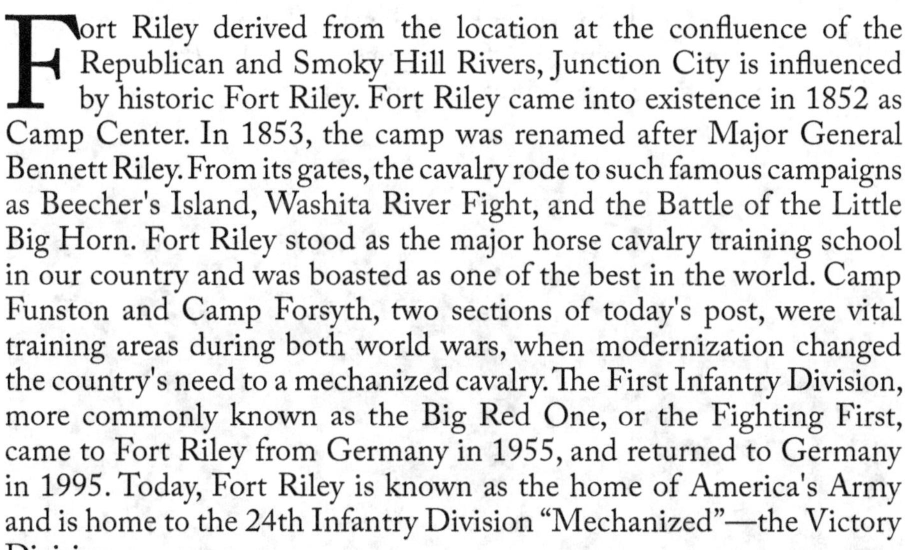

ort Riley derived from the location at the confluence of the Republican and Smoky Hill Rivers, Junction City is influenced by historic Fort Riley. Fort Riley came into existence in 1852 as Camp Center. In 1853, the camp was renamed after Major General Bennett Riley. From its gates, the cavalry rode to such famous campaigns as Beecher's Island, Washita River Fight, and the Battle of the Little Big Horn. Fort Riley stood as the major horse cavalry training school in our country and was boasted as one of the best in the world. Camp Funston and Camp Forsyth, two sections of today's post, were vital training areas during both world wars, when modernization changed the country's need to a mechanized cavalry. The First Infantry Division, more commonly known as the Big Red One, or the Fighting First, came to Fort Riley from Germany in 1955, and returned to Germany in 1995. Today, Fort Riley is known as the home of America's Army and is home to the 24th Infantry Division "Mechanized"—the Victory Division.

One hundred fifty years ago Fort Riley, Kansas was established as a post from which soldiers of the 7th Cavalry could protect people and goods moving over the Oregon and Santa Fe tails from Indian attacks. Today, the post is known as "America's War-fighting Center" and is home to elements of the 1st Armored and 1st Infantry divisions.

During the 1850s and into the Civil War period, the fort was a staging area for soldiers dispersed along overland trails and near settlements. In 1892, the Cavalry and Light Artillery School was built at Fort Riley and, later, the Mounted Service School focused on training individual soldiers and officers rather than regiments.

During that same period, the fort was selected as one of the installations to host the first large-scale combined maneuvers between regular and National Guard units. The United States' entry into World War I established Fort Riley as a divisional training center and resulted in the construction of Camp Funston, where the 10th and 89th divisions as well as elements of the 92nd Division trained. Between the wars, the fort again became a center for instruction, training, and summer camps.

After WWII, Fort Riley's Camp Forsyth became home to the Cavalry Replacement Training Center, and a rebuilt Camp Funston was used by armored divisions. The Army General Ground School was created and operated until 1950 to teach new officers such common military skills as map reading, company administration, and military law. The fort also operated one of the Army's first officer candidate schools.

During the Cold War years, Fort Riley was home to the Aggressor School. Similar to the opposing force concept of today, the "aggressors" provided a realistic "enemy" force for unit training.

The 10th Infantry Division was stationed at Fort Riley between 1948 and 1954 and conducted basic training for new recruits. In 1955, the post welcomed the 1st Inf. Div.

The "Big Red One" deployed soldiers to Southeast Asia in the mid-1960s, demonstrating that the post could equip, train, and deploy soldiers worldwide. More recently, soldiers of the 1st Infantry Division and other Fort Riley units deployed to the Persian Gulf region for Operations Desert Shield and Desert Storm in 1990 and 1991.

The Slaughters had reached their destination, noticing flat land scenery. There were no trees along the highway and no tall buildings. It's as if nothing were out there. The kids woke up and couldn't believe what they were seeing.

"Yep, y'all can wake up now, we are finally here. See the sign on that tower? The Big Red One. I'm here… boy, I don't see black people. I wonder how many blacks live out here."

"Honey, I don't see any either. Look at the historic buildings."

Carlos drove onto the Post, pulling up and parking at the In and Out Processing Center to check in on post. Virginia and the kids stayed in the car while Carlos entered the building. Carlos returned to the car with directions on how to get to the guest house. The family couldn't believe the scenery. Carlos arrived at the guest house and parked, entering the building to check on the procedures for checking in his family. Carlos returned and unloaded the car and family, escorting them inside. The family rooms were located upstairs in Carwell Guest House. The facility definitely was different from Fort Stewart. Rooms were small and they had to go down the hall to the kitchen to prepare their food. There were no kitchen areas in their rooms.

"Well, this is home for a while until we find us a place to stay. It shouldn't be that long to find us an apartment until we can get assigned on Post. The soldier at the In and Out Processing Center said that it takes at least one year to get Post Housing, and we probably will have to buy a house, but I'm going to check with housing tomorrow 'cause you can't believe what people say. Kids, what side of the room y'all want?

"Dad, Mom, Junior and I can sleep near the window!"

"It doesn't matter to me. I'm tired and ready to go to bed. At least they have adjoining rooms," Virginia said.

"Mom and Dad, can we go down stairs and check out the guest house?" Junior said.

"Okay, but don't stay long. Carlos, they saw those kids hanging out in the kitchen area."

"Yep, well at least we know our kids won't be bored. Apparently, there must be a lot of people processing into this place." Within an hour, Carlos left the room to fetch the kids while Virginia continued to unpack and call their family in Macon to confirm their safe arrival to Fort Riley. Carlos returned with the kids who were filled with conversation about the other kids they met in the kitchen who were also came from Germany. The kids also shared their feelings about the Christmas Holidays, saying it was nice to be among family and friends, but they prefer not to spend any more Christmas Holidays with family due to shortage or their receipt of gifts from their parents. Virginia explained to the kids that this is what happens when family moves in this time of year. Families cannot afford to buy their children a lot of gift due to no room for storage and travel finances. They family shower and change into their night gowns to rest. Carlos and Virginia reviewed their welcome package discussing their new environment.

The next day, Carlos went to sign into his new unit 2nd and 3rd ADA. The unit authorized Carlos time off to locate housing and enrolled his kids in local schools. Carlos returned to the hotel to pick up Virginia and the kids, so they can enroll the children into the local school. Carlene enrolled in Junction City High School, and Junior in the Junction City Middle School. The kids were excited to know their new environment. They had adjusted and were flexible to change. Once the Slaughters finished enrolling the kids, the next step was house hunting. They returned to the hotel to review their Welcome Package and local telephone directory.

Carlene and Junior were bored and wanted to tour the Post, so the family gathered their belongings and raced out of the Carwell Guest House to the Post. Virginia and the kids wanted to go the Post Exchange to check out the facility. Once the family arrived and entered the Post, they all realized that is was not stocked like the exchange in Germany, due to them having access to many competitive stores that would provide their domestic needs at low prices. The family purchased a few personal items and returned to the guest house. The kids wanted to visit their friends who they met the Sarvertson family.

Virginia gathered up the family laundry and headed to the laundry room to wash clothes. Virginia arrived in the Laundry room and she met Rosetta Sarvertson. They had a pleasant conversation discussing their adventure in Germany and how glad they were to be back in the United States among natives, especially the use of English language. They discussed their new challenges, networking for employment. This was always spouse's challenge—getting to know their new environment and building a new network for employment, but they will both visit Fort Riley's Civilian Personnel Advisory Center for assistance. They shared their employment history and wished each other luck. They also discussed house hunting indicating how they could believe this area didn't have many apartment vacancies and purchasing a house will be the final resolution in establishing a home. Both women were very excited because neither one of them had ever owned a home. After the women finished chatting and doing laundry, they returned to their rooms. Virginia shared to Carlos her conversation with Mrs. Sarvertson.

"Well, I'm glad you have met someone."

"I'm glad, too. Now, I won't be bored. Maybe Rosetta and I can get out and go shopping together and learn about our new environment. I haven't met her husband, but she seemed nice."

"Well, Dear, I'm going to get the kids so we can go and get something to eat. I'll be back." Carlos went downstairs in the lounge and met Sergeant Sarvertson while looking for his kids. The men discussed their new assignment at Fort Riley and how they can't wait to find a place to settle their families. Carlos gathered up his kids returned to their room to get Virginia, so they can go out to eat.

The next day, Carlos reported to PT formation and met with the unit Commander who told Slaughter, after running and exercises routine, Slaughter was excused from 9 a.m. formation to go house hunting. The Commander said that he had heard great things about Sergeant Slaughter and was glad to have him on board. Slaughter thanked the Commander for his assistance.

Slaughter returned back to the guest house and fetched Virginia and they went to Caldwell realtor in Junction City for assistance in finding a home. They wanted to live in Junction City and not Manhattan due to it was closer to Fort Riley, though everyone said that Manhattan was more developed than Junction City. The Slaughters realtor Heidi Marlow took them to see several houses. The Slaughters were shocked to see the cost and size of the homes. The Slaughters did not see any houses that were appealing to them. They did select one that they may consider out of the homes selections. The Slaughters returned to the hotel to share the news with the children who returned from school. Later that day, Virginia went to the kitchen to prepare a meal and Rosetta was present. The ladies shared their house hunting experiences, expressing how difficult it is to choose a house. Minutes later, Carlene and Junior ran into the kitchen to get permission to go with Rosetta's children to the Youth Center.

"Virginia, I didn't know Carlene and Junior were your kids!" Rosetta said.

"Yep. These are my kids!"

"Mom, please let us go!" Carlene said.

"Who all going?" Virginia asked.

"Leon is going to take my kids, and I'm quite sure he wouldn't mind your kids joining them," Rosetta said.

"Okay. Y'all better not get into any trouble!"

"Okay, Mom!" Carlene and Junior ran upstairs to get their coats.

The children told Carlos about Virginia giving them permission to go to the Youth Center with Mr. Salverston. Junior asked his father if he want to go to the Youth Center. Carlos decided to join, grabbing his belongings and stopping by the kitchen to tell Virginia. They immediately rushed downstairs to meet Leon.

"How many children do you have, Rosetta?"

"I have three. Roger, oldest and the same age as Carlene; Leroy, same age as Junior; and Juanita. Girl, they will be just fine. Leon will be staying with the kids."

"Okay. I know the kids are getting bored hanging around this hotel!

Leon and Carlos took the kids to the Youth Center and discovered there was a basketball game at King Field House, 1sdt Brigade verse 2nd and 3rd ADA. The kids heard Sergeant Booth telling them about the game and start yelling can we go Dad. So, Leon and Carlos change their plans and went to the basketball game. Leon and Carlos arrived at King Field House mingling among their colleagues cheering for Slaughter's unit.

Leon and Carlos returned with the kids saying that they had a good time. The kids agreed requesting to go again with Mr. Leon. Leon entered the Slaughter room to chat with Carlos. They discussed the unit and Fort Riley. They also talked about the stress of finding a house and how they could not wait to get settled. They both agreed that they did not want to stay in the area after they retire. The want to find a house that would easily sell when the time come for them to depart the area.

CHAPTER THREE

MOVE TO JUNCTION CITY

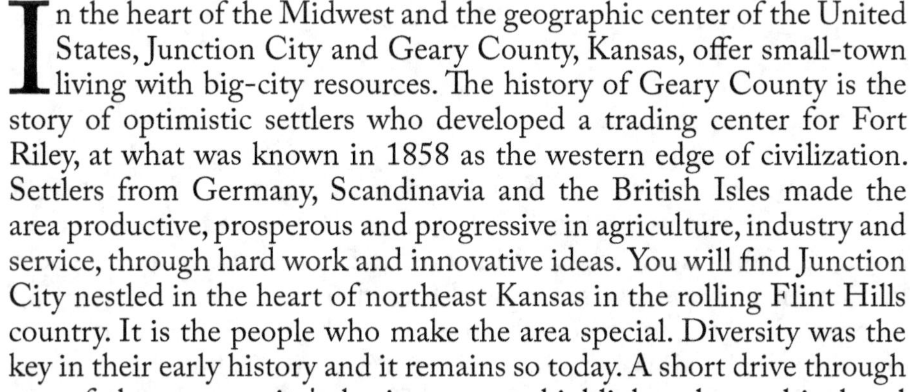

In the heart of the Midwest and the geographic center of the United States, Junction City and Geary County, Kansas, offer small-town living with big-city resources. The history of Geary County is the story of optimistic settlers who developed a trading center for Fort Riley, at what was known in 1858 as the western edge of civilization. Settlers from Germany, Scandinavia and the British Isles made the area productive, prosperous and progressive in agriculture, industry and service, through hard work and innovative ideas. You will find Junction City nestled in the heart of northeast Kansas in the rolling Flint Hills country. It is the people who make the area special. Diversity was the key in their early history and it remains so today. A short drive through any of the community's business areas highlights the multicultural makeup of the area.

Sitting next to Junction City, Milford Lake is the largest man-made lake in Kansas. Milford Lake was authorized by Congress in 1954 and constructed by the Corps of Engineers in the early 1960s. It provides flood control, navigation, improved water quality, water supply, recreation, plus fish and wildlife benefits; an average of a half million people visit Milford Lake each year. Eleven parks offer camping, picnicking, swimming, boat ramps, and fishing access. Approximately 23,000 acres are managed for wildlife and hunting opportunities.

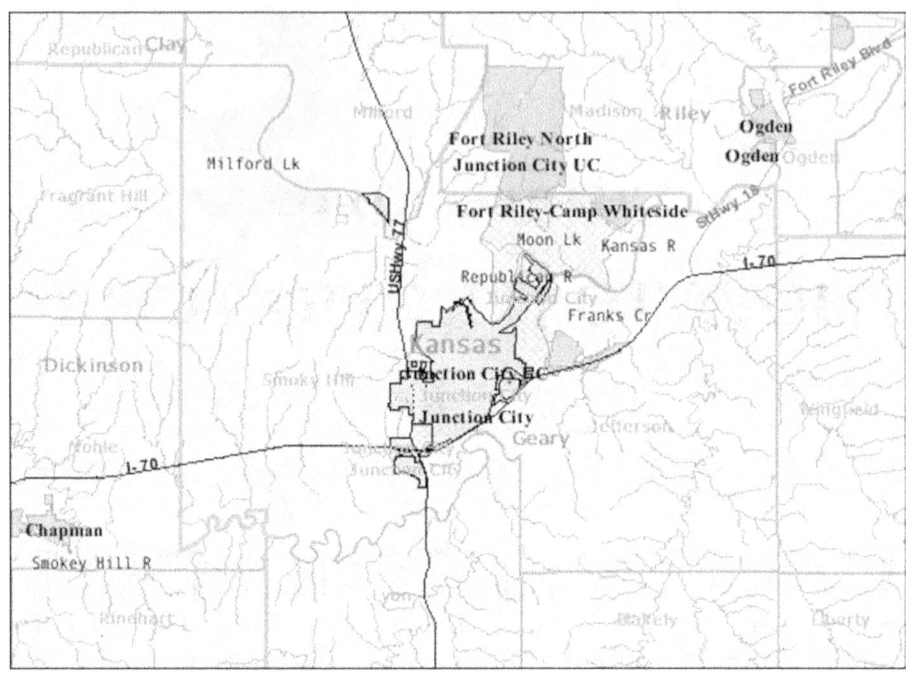

Within four weeks, the Slaughters and Salvertsons found them a home and moved to the Junction City area. They were both concerned about receiving their household goods and hoped the damage would be minimal. The Slaughters moved into their home and the moving company brought their households goods. There were some damages and they filed claims for reimbursement and repair, but overall, their household goods survived the four years storage with limited damages. Carlene, Carlos, and Junior were amazed at the accumulation of furniture, figurines, and other household goods Virginia had purchased. Their four bedrooms, family room, kitchen, three baths and dining room house were fully furnished.

"Mom. Now I know why you did all that shopping! You were preparing for this day when we moved into our home." Carlene said.

"Yep. Now you see! There is no way we could afford a home and furnish it without struggling. That's why you saw mama making a list as we visited other countries, because I had a vision of how I wanted to decorate my home and it has finally come true. Dreams will come true if you have faith in yourself and family."

"Mom, I'm going to do just like you did when I get ready to buy my home."

The Slaughters spent weeks housekeeping and decorating. Everyone was pleased, but the kids wished they had a pool. Virginia was glad she did not have to worry about the kids' safety, even if they did know how to swim. The Slaughters discovered some household damages and submitted their claims to the Fort Riley Transportation Department. Virginia was amazed that their Asian furniture only had minor damages. She applied motor oil to all of them because of the tips from her housemaid when they were in Okinawa, and the furniture did not have any mole or major damages. She decided to continue treating all her wood furniture by applying oil weekly and only applying oil once every four to six months thanks to those tips.

Months had passed and Virginia became bored being just a domestic engineer and started on getting a job. She submitted her application to the local CPAC and waited to hear from the agency. Meanwhile, she decided to fulfill her dreams of writing a novel. The family was excited to hear the news, especially Carlos. He knew that his wife was bored, and writing would fill that boredom until she found a job. HE ensured that she had all the equipment she needed to get started. Virginia was focused on writing her novel. She would take materials to Milford Lake for family gathering to capture ideas. Carlene took an interest in her writing, reading her mother's manuscripts and expressing her feelings of approval. She especially became excited when she read the manuscript, realizing it was about their life living among the military community.

Virginia visited the Library and bookstores to gain information on how to submit her manuscript once it was finished. She had come across so many spouses and families who had problems coping with their marriage, among other family issues. Virginia decided that she wanted to share her blessings and knowledge with the world, which lead to writing her story and other novels relating to family issues. So, during her spare time, she wrote several manuscripts, found a literacy agent, and submitted her manuscripts. Carlene was very proud and could not believe her mother's new-found talent, hoping one day that her mother's dream of becoming an author would come true.

A month later, Carlos ran across a colleague who was stationed in Berlin and a member of Order of Eastern Star, Sergeant First Class Carla Spivey. They chatted about Berlin and Fort Riley. Spivey wanted to see Virginia and asked Carlos about the Auxiliaries in their area. They had not visited any Masonic Auxiliary and decided that it was time to and become active. So, Carlos gave Spivey with his telephone number, mailing address and got Spivey's contact as well, so he could visit her in Abilene. That afternoon, Carlos returned home sharing the news of running into Spivey. That following weekend, the Slaughters visited Spivey. Carla and Virginia talked of their adventures in Berlin and their point of views about Fort Riley, saying that there is nothing to do, and in order to shop, they have to drive thirty to forty-five minutes to the nearest mall in Manhattan and Topeka. Carla said that she had information about the Eastern Star chapter meetings in Junction City and invited Virginia to join her in attending. Carlos and Fred Spivey joined the ladies who were sitting outside in the yard, they told them it was time for them to head back to Junction City. Carla told Virginia that she will call to let her know when the next meeting will be.

Carla called Virginia and gave her the schedule of the Eastern Star meetings. The ladies attended and were disappointed on how the chapters in the States conducted their meetings. But realized they were not among active military members. The members were civilian and retired military, and meetings were conducted differently. The ladies were knowledgeable and ready to face the challenges the chapter offered. The members also provided their newcomers with information on local churches. Many of the chapter members attend Second Missionary Baptist Church and invited the new comers to visit the church services. Virginia and her family visited many churches included Second Missionary Baptist Church. Carlos and Virginia were very pleased with Second Missionary Baptist services. They both decided that this will be the church worshiping selection for their family.

Virginia called Rosetta and told her about attending the Eastern Star meeting and discovered that Rosetta was a member and invited her to attend the meetings. The ladies continued to go to their meetings and eventually joined the local Eastern Star Masonic Auxiliary.

Carlos and Leon would have cookouts on the weekends rotating among each other inviting soldiers from their units, among family and friends. Carlos had a cookout at his house and invited Spivey, Salvertson, and soldiers in his unit. Carlos and Leon prepared the meat on the grill and the ladies brought their side dishes. The ladies joined the men out in the backyard, chatting about Kansas and how bored they were when Fred stumbled across the lawn chair, saying that he was going to leave Kansas. "I hate Fort Riley and I can't wait to leave. I can't find a job and living in Abilene in the middle of nowhere is killing me." Fred was from Baltimore and loved living in the city. He couldn't adjust to living in a rural area where he had to drive for miles to get to a mall or downtown to the clubs. He didn't like the clubs in the area either and drank himself to death.

Carla told Fred to sit down, saying that nobody wants to hear how bored he is. "I told you that I'm trying to get reassigned due to my mother's illness."

"Well. You better get reassigned or you will be by yourself. I can't take this anymore, and I'm looking to leave next month, and you and the kids can stay in Kansas."

"Fred... I know you would not leave your wife and children out here by themselves. You're just talking trash 'cause you've had a few drinks," Rosetta said.

"No! I mean it! I'm leaving Carla and the kids. This is her damn career. I've tried to hang in there and every time I get me a good job, she comes down on an assignment and we have to leave. Now, Germany— loved it! A man can only take so much, but here, I hate it and I got to go."

"Carlos! Carlos! Come talk to Fred. You don't drink.

Maybe you can talk some sense into him."

"Fred, come help me and Leon take the meat off the grill!" Carlos said.

With a beer in hand, Fred stumbled around the ladies, walking over to help the guys at the grill. "Carlos, I mean it man. I'm leaving Carla. I'm drinking more than I ever drank before and it's getting on her nerves."

"Man, Carla even drinks a couple of beers and she never drink after work. It's this place and it's time to go."

"Well, I know how you feel, but we're going to make the best of this tour. You see, I stay busy and get involved in sports, like hunting and fishing. To tell you the truth, I like it here.

"Well, Man, y'all can have it! I'm gone. Just as soon as next month, I'm out of here!"

Carla told Rosetta and Virginia she had put in to be reassigned and was sure that it will be approved. Carla hated Fort Riley and living in Abilene just made it worst. She said that it probably wouldn't be as bad if she lived on Post, but it takes at least a year or more, and she could not afford to buy a house and she did not want to purchase a home in this area. Now, she wishes that she didn't purchased that Volvo and then maybe their budget would not be as tight. Rosetta mentioned to Virginia that she noticed that they both were doing some heavy drinking and she knows Virginia is glad Carlos didn't drink. Virginia concurred with Rosetta and both ladies felt sadness for the Spivey family. Carla brought up the National Training Center where the units went to California to train for a month. Rosetta and Virginia both hated that the guys had to go but knew that it was a part of the guys career for training. At least the training was for one month and the ladies can manage without their husband for a month. The guys on the other hand, dreaded going to NTC were wishing that they didn't have to go and were not looking forward to leaving their families. Rosetta and Virginia said at least they know one another and the unit did have Military Wives support groups. During that summer, Virginia was stricken with an illness of possible breast cancer. She discovered a lump during her breast self-examination and shared this with Carlos. They both were worried and didn't know what to expect. Virginia's physician at Irwin Army Community Hospital scheduled her for a biopsy. The surgery included removing the lump and testing for cancer. Virginia became very nervous. She didn't know what to do. She constantly looked in the mirror visioning herself without her breast and she became frightened facing reality. Carlos attended Virginia's doctor appointment, providing support and encouraging his wife to be strong and to have faith. The doctor scheduled Virginia a same-day surgery in Out Patient Clinic. Carlos stood by Virginia until she rolled into the surgery room. Two hours passed, though it seemed longer to Carlos. When the physician came out into the lobby, he notified Carlos that Virginia is alright and it's not cancer. Apparently, his wife has fibroid cysts in her left breast. The doctor said that they removed the fibroid cysts and that Virginia will be in pain for a couple weeks and scheduled her a follow-up appointment. Carlos shouted for joy, praising God for sparing his wife from cancer. Carlos immediately asked if he can see his wife, and the doctor said that she will be out in a few minutes. The physician said that Virginia will be held in the treatment room for observation and if her vital signs are normal, she will be released. Carlos rushed to his wife's bedside, waiting patiently for her dismissal.

Virginia awoke, Carlos asked what the doctor said and he told her the news—no cancer. Minutes later, the doctor came in and released Virginia. Virginia held on to Slaughter's hands. Carlos, with tears in his eyes, said God is good. Slaughter assisted his wife getting dressed. Together, they exited the hospital. The kids were glad to see Virginia when they came home and hear the news. The Slaughters faced a challenge again and survived the stress.

CHAPTER FOUR

THE SLAUGHTERS GOOD NEWS

Carla called Virginia to share her good news that she has been reassigned to Fort Monmouth, New Jersey. This is the assignment that Carla and her family wanted and it happened. Virginia very happy for Carla and hoped that she and Fred will be a family again. Carla was not sure what this meant about saving her marriage, but she was happy because this was home for her, and she would have assistance in raising her boys. Carla only had three years and she would be eligible for retirement.

Carlos saw Carla at the Post Exchange and she told him the news. She said that she will not be going to NTC because she will do a permanent change of station to Fort Monmouth. Carlos returned to his unit and began to prepare for NTC deployment. Carlos was one of the best NCO 2/3 ADA had as a soldier. He ensured that all equipment and material was available for the units' deployment. Carlos was not only concerned about the unit being equipped for deployment, but assisted his soldiers in making sure they were physically and mentally ready. Carlos had a white soldier, SPC Simpson, who had family problems and did not want to go to NTC. The soldier revealed that he had some domestic issues, and Carlos suspected that this soldier had a drinking problem. Carlos reached out to the Simpson, giving him support and advice. He told him to consider getting help dealing with his drinking and no matter how heated up his domestic issues become, not to physically harm his spouse. He also helped the soldier with getting his finances under control by referring him to local agency and ensuring he received good assistance from the Army Community Services. Two weeks later, Carlos received a call from Simpson's parents, thanking him for going out of his way to assist their son. Carlos was a sergeant who always reached out to assist his soldiers' either financially or he directed them to their local resources.

One week prior to the troops departing for NTC, the unit sponsored a trip for the soldiers and their family to go to Worlds of Fun amusement park. Carlos signed his family up for this event. The unit provided bus transportation, but Carlos and Sergeant First Class Wright decided to drive, so they can leave when their family was ready. The soldiers gathered at the unit, those who were riding the bus boarded the bus and those driving lined up behind the bus with maps providing direction to Worlds of Fun. The convoy departed from Fort Riley heading for the Worlds of Fun. While driving on I-70, Wright drove along the highway positioning his car in the left lane.

"Hey, man, what's up? Don't forget to wait for us when you get to the park and I do the same for you," Write said.

"Alright, sound good to me," Carlos said.

The convoy arrived at Worlds of Fun gate and processed into the park. The Slaughters and Wright joined together and enjoyed their day at the park. Carlos took pictures of his family and soldiers while they all enjoyed their day at the park. While taking pictures, Carlos overhears his wife and daughter mentioned Virginia's dream vacations a cruise to the Bahamas, but Virginia states that this is a fun trip too.

Carlos and Virginia joined the children riding on the Roller Coaster, Water Log Ride, and other rides throughout the park joining hands with their children and friends. Carlos would kiss periodically while strolling through the park. Junior and Carlene would smile, teasing their parents calling them lovebirds.

"Don't you all know how much I love my wife and there is nothing wrong with kissing, expressing my love," Carlos said.

"Dad, we are just teasing you guys," the kids said.

They were very happy to see their parents together and enjoying the park. This day adventure definitely was very relaxing for the families assigned to 2 and 3rd ADA. The time had arrived for the Slaughters to depart the park and return to Junction City.

The Slaughter family prepared for Carlos going to NTC. Virginia and kids hated the fact that Carlos had to go on this essential training exercise. Carlos and his family gather Carlos things, loaded up their vehicle, and took Carlos to the Unit for departure to NTC. When the family arrived, they immediately stood among the rest of soldiers' family saying farewell. Carlos told Virginia to keep in touch with the commander's wife who will provide the wives with information and assistance during the soldiers' absence. Carlos embraced his family and kissed them, told them to take care and he will call once he gets a chance.

Virginia and the kids returned home saying how much they miss Carlos. Virginia told the kids that Carlos is only going to be gone approximately a month. Meanwhile, they must be strong and they must behave until Carlos returns. Junior said Carlos told him he is the man of the house until he's back0. Every night, Junior ensured that the doors were locked before he went to bed because that's what his dad did every night, and he's in charge until he returns. Virginia just looked at Junior as she admired the role he honored during the absence if his father.

A week later, Carlos called home to inform the family that he was alright and the training is going smoothly. He said that it's very hot and he missed the family and couldn't wait until he could return home. Virginia told Slaughter that she had a special surprise waiting for him. Carlos said that the only thing he wanted was Virginia and could not wait to be back in her arms again. Virginia and kids were deeply involved in their special project, staining the cabinet in the kitchen and attending Junior's basketball games. Junior told his mom that Carlos is going to be surprised when he sees the kitchen. Virginia agreed with her son and told them they are doing a great job assisting her. Moments later, Virginia received a call from her farther inviting them to the upcoming family reunion. Virginia told him that they will be there and that she just received a letter from her Class Reunion Committee announcing the reunion, which is scheduled the same weekend of the Cottingham's family reunion.

A month later, the soldiers were returning from NTC and families gathered at the unit waiting. Virginia and the kids, along with other families, decorated the unit supply room and outside entrance, welcoming the soldiers. The soldiers arrived, and Carlos was happy to see his family among the crowd. "I didn't expect y'all to be here. I thought I would have to call you to pick me up. How did you find out when we will be at the unit?"

"Well, Dear, you have the commander's wife to thank. She coordinates this special "welcome home" event.

"Man, I'm glad she did this. Boy, this is nice."

The Slaughters joined in with the crowd to welcome the soldiers back and, later, Carlos gather his things and drove his family home. When he arrived, Virginia and kids had decorated the home, welcoming Carlos back. Carlos was pleased to see how much his family missed him and raced to the shower to change so he could enjoy them. While Carlos was showering, Virginia rushed to the kitchen to get her special surprise, a romantic cool whip treat, and took it in their bedroom. She lit the candles for their special night. When Carlos finished showering, the kids guided him to the kitchen and asked if he saw anything different. Carlos noticed the cabinet was varnished. He said that they did a good job. Kissing and hugging everyone. They also mention the Cottinghams family's upcoming reunion, yelling about wanting to go, which Carlos said approved and told the kids to take their bath. The kids went downstairs to bathe and dress for bed. Minutes later, Carlos went downstairs to tuck the kids in bed while Virginia showered and changed for bed. Carlos returned to the bedroom after tucking the kids in bed, and Virginia guided Carlos to their bedroom so they can make passionate love all night.

Two days passed and Carlos returned to work, rounding up his troops departing for the Unit Motor Pool to clean up their vehicles. The troops were all in good spirit and excited to be home. Carlos was a soldier that always ensured safety and found easy methods on how to complete the tasks on time. He told the troops in the Motor Pool that their Unit Inspection will be next on their agenda, so it was very important that they clean all unit vehicles to meet the inspection regulations guidelines. Carlos worked along with his troops. After the troops had finished, Carlos released the troops to go home early. One of Carlos troops suggested they go and celebrate at the NCO club. Carlos said that whatever they do with their time off was up to them, but advised the soldiers especially those with families to consider taking this time to be with their families, because that's exactly what he was going to do and encourage others with families to do the same thing. In the early years in Carlos's career, he would have hung out with his fellow soldiers, but the new Carlos, enjoys spending every moment with his family.

Two months later, the Slaughters received a call from Hamilton Literacy Agency informing the family that they will publish Virginia's novel. The representative, Mr. Carl Scott, told Virginia that he loved the manuscript and she definitely had the talent. He also shared that he was going through a divorce and had a special interest in the manuscript and will be the editor. The representative told Virginia that he will be contacting Virginia to review the editing of both manuscripts before they are submitted to a publishing company. Carlos was shocked to hear the news. They shared the news with the kids. This was a beginning of a new career for Virginia. Carlos kissed Virginia saying how proud he was of her.

The next day, Virginia attended the Eastern Star meeting, and Darlene Hopkins, one of the members, who worked at Irwin Army Community Hospital told Virginia that she made the referral list and someone will be contacting her soon. Virginia realized that being active in the Auxiliary is a great communication networking system. It was not always the knowledge, skills, and abilities that will give assistance in obtaining a job but establishing network in knowing people within the community is a great tool to ensure your goals for employment.

Weeks later, Virginia was contacted for an interview and selected for a Medial Clerk position at the hospital. Virginia has to accept a downgrade in pay, but she finally got back into Civil Service. When Carlos arrived home, Virginia shared the good news about getting the job at IACH. Carlos was happy for his wife saying now it's time for me to get a second vehicle. Carlos purchased a truck from one of his soldiers who received orders assigned to Germany. At the next Eastern Star meeting, Virginia thanked Darlene for her assistance in obtaining this job. The ladies planned a farewell dinner Slaughters' home for Carla who was going to Fort Monmouth at the. All the Eastern Star members joined together to wish Carla farewell.

During that year, Junior joined the Middle School football team. The Slaughters gathered as a family to attend all of Junior's games.

While attending one of Junior's football practice, Virginia met Cynthia Banner. Cynthia had a son playing football and the ladies began to chat about their tour in Germany. Virginia discovered that Cynthia was member of Eastern Star of Oklahoma Jurisdictions but is not active, so Virginia invited her to come out to one of their meetings.

Virginia loved her job working at the hospital and was elected into an officer seat as Associate Worthy Matron in the Order of the Eastern Stars. Virginia's life was full of joy, laughter and promises to explore her goals toward a successful future. During that year, Junior became headline news in sports and Virginia became headlines for the Eastern Star in the *Daily Union*. The Slaughters became well-known among the Junction City community. But that was not the only talent Virginia took to heights. Virginia's position working at the hospital added the touch of quality services to the patients seen in the Outpatient Clinic. Working as a team, Virginia, Veronica, Cheryl, and Anita ranked the highest performance of all the clerks of the Outpatient Clinic. Veronica's favorite words when the storm would come rushing in were "all right now, I don't want mess," and she would process those patient appointments and keep our supervisor in line. Anita words were "Why change if our system is working?"

Virginia's knowledge lead to the discovery of abuse to Equal Employment Opportunity for all Medical employees at IACH. One day, Virginia realized that the clerks' job description did not apply to the Medical Clerks performing duties, so she shared this information with Cheryl Farmer and together they worked as a team to get the position upgraded. Virginia had her work cut out for her, but she never feared a challenge. Together, Cheryl and Virginia presented their case to the Union and fought the battle to upgrade the positions. But that was not the only challenge Virginia had to deal with. She was elected at the election for next year's Worthy Matron, President of Order of the Eastern Star Auxiliary.

This was a challenging year for the Slaughters. Carlene was a senior and Junior was a freshman at Junction City High School. Junior and Virginia continued to make the headline in the *Daily Union* in sporting events and organization Fund Raiser Events. One of Virginia's fund raiser projects was sponsoring a fashion show that was held at the VFW in Ogden, Kansas. This event made headline in the *Daily Union*. The event included modeling of all fashion attire, Business, Casual, Sport, Lingerie, and Formal ware. The event provided scenes that inspirationally sparked attraction for the audience to encourage purchasing the products and entertainment. The highlights of the show were presentations, acknowledgement honoring the Grand Worthy Matron Anna Horton and commentator Virginia. Virginia spoke words of expression as she presented the fashion designs, which move the audience. Carlos would sit and stand among the crowd taking pictures at every event Virginia sponsored supporting her goals of success. One would say like Mother, like son because the Slaughters' name was definitely in the news.

During the year of 1993, Junior was elected the Junction City High School Sophomore King for the Homecoming game and Queen was Pillar Woodard. The Slaughters attend the games and joined the fans to cheer for victory for the team. Virginia, Carlene, and Carlos were very proud of Junior as they sat among the crowd cheering for victory. Carlene couldn't believe that her brother was elected and stationed herself on the field to support her brother's victorious night. Junior's fame didn't stop as King for the homecoming, but continued in basketball scoring high point during the game. The Slaughters spent a lot of time supporting Junior attending his games and enjoyed watching their son perform on the court. They would seat among the audience in the gym applauding his victorious games. Junior acquired the talent to participate in all sports, but Carlos and Virginia would only allow him to participate in basketball and baseball. This way, during his sophomore year, he could focus on maintaining his grade to complete his high school academic requirements.

During this year, Virginia and Carlene faced the challenge of womanhood. Carlene obtained employment working at Dillon Food Store as a cashier. Carlene also had to face the pressure in dating. Their relationship changed from mother and daughter to friends, but Virginia did not lose sight of her position as parent for Carlene. In fact, their new-found relationship enhanced a quality of security for Carlene, knowing that she could share all her problems with her mother and not be embarrassed to share her intimate crisis. One of their most challenging experiences was birth control. Carlene asked advise from Virginia, and she assisted her daughter to see a gynecologist. Virginia was amazed at the courage Carlene revealed when she had her first Pap smear, and Virginia discovered that her daughter was still a virgin who sought her mother for guidance as she approached womanhood. Virginia also spent time teaching both Carlene and Junior how to drive. Carlos provided his assistance, which was limited due to late hours working. Carlene enrolled in the Driver's Ed Class to prepare to get her driver's license. Together they discussed the preparation of Carlene becoming a responsible young adult. Three months later, Carlene got her license. Carlos and Virginia noticed how responsible Carlene was driving Virginia's car and decided it was time for Carlene to have her own car.

The Cottinghams were having their family reunion so the Slaughters traveled to Macon to participate in this event. This also was the Fifteen Class Reunion event being held in Macon. Mr. Cottingham was very glad to have his daughter to join this event. Virginia finally got the opportunity to meet the family that she had heard so much about, but never got the opportunity to chat with them. This event was held in Perry, Georgia, at the Holiday Inn. They had a cookout at the local park; eating, dancing, playing games, and laughing and chatting among friends and family. Mr. Cottingham told Virginia that he had divorced Helen, which saddened Virginia, but she saw happiness in her father's eyes. Virginia mingled with the family discovering the history of the white man blood that run through her veins. She was told by her parents that her great grandfather was white and a judge of Killeen, Georgia, and this explained the light-colored skin and grayish eyes that were common in the Cottingham family. The family spoke of how proud Judge Cottingham was of his children, grandchildren, and great grandchildren, and his struggle of freedom fought for his family. Virginia, Tricia, Shawn, Carlene and the rest of family danced the evening away to the music of DJ Johnson. Carlos, Mr. Cottingham, his brother, and uncle stood alongside, observing, and chatting as they dance the night away.

The time had come for them to leave and returned to the hotel. Virginia and Carlos checked on her mother who didn't attend due to illness when she returned to the kid's room and chat about how much fun they had and wish her mother could have joined them. Mrs. Cottingham just listened as her daughter chatted with her family. Carlene told her grandmother about Junior's interest in dating white girls. The subject didn't surprise Mrs. Cottingham, because she told Carlene that Junior will be the one to bring white race among the next generation.

The next day, Mrs. Cottingham, Carlos, Virginia, and kids had breakfast with the family at the hotel dining room. Mr. Cottingham was glad to see his ex-wife feeling better. Mrs. Cottingham was glad to be among her children as they explore their first family reunion.

That evening, Virginia and Carlos dressed to attend their Class Reunion promising to be back at the hotel for the dining out event with the family. They arrived at the Garden Inn Lounge in Macon where the event was held and mingled among their classmates. Everyone looked different—mature—and chatted about their challenges and success. Virginia and Carlos notice that a lot of classmates were missing and asked the rest of their whereabouts. Charles mentioned that Larry was married and living in Atlanta. Later that night, Ellie came in with her significant other. Virginia heard that she had married, divorced, and had an eleven-year-old daughter. Ellie and her escort saw Carlos and Virginia and decided to join them at their table.

"Hi, Carlos and Virginia. What have you all been doing? I heard that you all were going to attend. Boy, y'all definitely looking different. What? It's been twenty years since we saw each other. So, tell me, are you all still traveling? I heard Carlos was stationed in Kansas."

Virginia a smiled and looked radiant as ever. "Yes, that's right, we are stationed at Fort Riley."

"I'm sorry. let me introduce you to my friend, Harold Davidson. These are my classmates Virginia and Carlos, high school sweethearts. Do you all mine if we sit at the table with you?"

"Oh, no! Go ahead. My name is Carlos." Carlos shook Harold's hands.

"My name is Harold!" He shook both Virginia's and Carlos's hand while assisting Ellie to her seat.

"So, Virginia, tell me, what you been going on in your life?"

"Nothing much, just enjoying married life, travelling, and, of course, working. And, oh. I forgot to mention my new-found talent, writing. Matter of fact, I have written several manuscripts that are waiting to be published."

The women continued to chat about their life while the guys talked about their adventures. Ellie changed the topic, referring to the past and revealing her relationship with Carlos. She said that she never had a relationship with Carlos and wanted to clear the air with Virginia who, for so many years, thought that her best friend had betrayed her. The ladies laughed and put their past behind them.

Carlos and Virginia realized it was getting late, and they had another engagement they need to attend, so they departed and drove back to the hotel. They went to the dining room, and everyone had eaten and left. So, they went to her father's room and he was lying in the bed, appearing to be ill, but didn't mention it. He said he was glad they came to the family reunion. Virginia embraced her father. She and Slaughter headed for the kids' room. Carlos forgot his glasses and left them at Mr. Cottingham room to retrieve them. Meanwhile, Virginia talked with her mother and Carlene when she discovered that Carlene had a vision of horses with wings flying over her mother as she was sleeping. Carlene said that she was not sleep and swore on the Bible she saw it. Virginia refused to believe Carlene then her mother spoke.

"Virginia, you need to listen to Carlene. She is telling the truth. Carlene has the gift to see the future. I know you won't t believe it, but when Carlene mentioned what she saw, I knew she wasn't lying."

"What does this mean?"

"I have no idea, but I know your daughter saw something, and it frighten her. I told my granddaughter not to be scared and have faith in God."

Carlos returned to the kids' room to get Virginia, and they went to their suite to discuss their night. Virginia expressed how much she loves Carlos and talked of her parents' health issues. Carlos discussed the class reunion and asked Virginia about her in-depth conversation with Ellie. He said he hope Ellie didn't upset her. Virginia assured Carlos that Ellie didn't upset her, neither could she say anything to destroy their love that will last forever. They kissed passionately and made love.

Virginia and her family checked out of the hotel the next day, returning to Macon. That same week, Virginia took her mother to a doctor appointment and discovered that her mother had not had a routine checkup. The doctors gave Mrs. Cottingham medicine to treat her illness of diabetes and high blood pressure. Virginia asked her mother to come back with her to Kansas. But, as usual, Mrs. Cottingham refused. The next day, Virginia's cousin Lisa called to mention Mr. Cottingham was ill. Virginia and Tricia rushed from Mrs. Cottingham's home and drove to visit Mr. Cottingham. He appeared to be in great pain and Virginia encouraged her father to go to the emergency room. They arrived at the emergency room escorting Mr. Cottingham to the registration desk. Mr. Cottingham noticed how attractive the receptionist look and started flirting. Virginia couldn't believe what she saw, and Tricia said he does this all the time when he sees a pretty woman.

"Now, you see for yourself, how daddy reacts with women."

"Yep, I do. He's forgotten all about his illness. I just can't believe what I'm seeing."

"Girl, that's our daddy. He loves women!"

"Well, I guess we will be here for a while, so we might as well have a seat. At least, we know that he's alright and getting treated for his illness. Every time, I come home, there is always something going on."

"Yep, and your dad is good at getting you to visit him when you are here."

"But you know Tricia, dad calls me all the time since he's not with Helen."

"You know how Helen is. She is something else. Did dad tell you how he found a briefcase full of money hidden up under her son's bed? Scared him to death because he didn't know what to do! That's when he confronted Helen, and she claimed she didn't know anything. Dad said that was when he decided to leave. He didn't know what they were doing or where the money came from, but he was not about to get caught in that mess. It probably was something illegal, but dad left and hasn't been back.

"No! Dad hasn't mentioned anything to me about that… but I'm glad he left!"

Mr. Cottingham was examined and the girls drove their father back home. They got Mr. Cottingham settled and prepared him a meal. Tricia said that he enjoyed them nursing him and Mr. Cottingham admitted it's true. Mr. Cottingham retrieved his Federal Employee Group Life Insurance. He told his daughters that, upon his death, this policy is divided among all his children. He also made the girls promise to purchase an item that will remind them of him. Mr. Cottingham knew that he didn't contribute to their financial needs when the girls were children. He only contributed what the courts enforced—his child support payment.

"Dad, why are you speaking about this now? You know I don't want to discuss what if s about your death. Besides, I'm not living in Macon, so you need to leave a copy with Tricia or Bro."

"I know you don't live here, and you don't want to discuss my death, but I want you all to know, and, Virginia, you are the person who will have to process this since you are working for the government."

"Okay, Dad, I'll listen, but I want you to give a copy to Tricia or Bro and leave a copy in your files."

Mr. Cottingham gave the girls a lecture about his required death arrangement. The girls left once he was settled. Virginia dropped Tricia off and picked Carlene up and went to visit with Ms. Slaughter's before they depart for Kansas, assuring her mother that she will return to say good-bye. The next day, the Slaughters said their good-byes to all their families and returned to Junction City.

A month later, Carlos presented his daughter with her very own car. Carlene was so excited to get an escort. She couldn't believe that her parents would do this. She jumped and hugged everyone. Carlos went for a drive with his daughter to ensure that she was familiar with the car. He mentioned to Carlene how proud he was of her and apologized for his limited time teaching her how the drive, but she has learned and this was her first car. Carlene replied saying that she understood her father's absence in spending time with his family due to his career. They returned from their drive and Virginia looked from the garage admiring the joy in her daughter's eyes.

Carlos walked towards Virginia. "You did a great job teaching Carlene how to drive."

"No. *We* did a great job, even though you had to work long hours and couldn't participate sometimes."

Months later, Virginia and Cheryl were up to their ears attending meetings presenting their case along with their Union Representative, Brittina. Virginia was the spoke person for the case and processed the paperwork. Virginia, Cheryl, and the Union Representative met with hospital representative to discuss their negotiation settlement. They worked very hard and their performance was excellent, so the hospital representative had no alternative but to grant the ladies their promotions. But Brittana didn't stop there. She wanted to pursue the issue further to get all Medical Clerks a promotion and the girls motivation, knowledge, and assistance lead to victory for all Medical Clerks. Again, Virginia was a part of a victorious challenge not only for herself, but others.

The Alfred P. Murrah Building just minutes after the "worst act of terrorism on American soil," which murdered 168 and injured more than 500 innocent persons on April 19, 1995.

Shortly after the bombing of the Murrah building, Yossef Bodansky, executive director of the Congressional Task Force on Terrorism and Unconventional Warfare, pieced together intelligence data strongly indicating that Islamic veterans of the 1979-89 Afghan war with the Soviet Union, who trained under Osama bin Laden, were responsible for the 1993 bombing of the World Trade Center and the Oklahoma federal building.

During the year 1995, two federal law enforcement agencies had information before the 1995 Oklahoma City bombing suggesting that white supremacists living nearby were considering an attack on government buildings. After the Oklahoma City bombing, FBI investigators gathered evidence linking Timothy McVeigh to white supremacists who had threatened to attack government buildings. The investigation leads the FBI to IACH due to Timothy McVeigh background employment history, which revealed prior Army military enlistment and who probably was a patient at IACH. Virginia and Cheryl was receptionist in questions by FBI authorities. They were the receptionist on duty during the time Timothy McVeigh and Terr y McNichols were seen as patients. The women provided the FBI assistance information from the IACH patient's software. The investigation also revealed evidence that Timothy McVeigh and Terr y McNichols plans to bomb Oklahoma federal building included purchasing a U-haul rental vehicle from a Rental company located in Junction City, Kansas. This event puts Junction City, Kansas City in the news nationwide.

After winning her case, Virginia turns her focus to the Eastern Stars. At the meeting, Virginia was told the ladies had issues about the Worthy Patron input in advising Virginia on how to conduct meetings and her relationship with the Worthy Patron. Virginia firmly addressed to the ladies her positioned and goals for the Order of Eastern Stars and indicated that they would not discuss anything personal, but keep it professional relationship between them and wanted the rumor to stop. Darlene concurs with Virginia. Virginia addressed the issue and conduct of women approving the Worthy Patron rights of providing advice to her on an as needed basis during the meeting. Apparently, the older members did not want a male to have input in making decisions, but Virginia brought a change, visibility among the community and increased the profits of the OES financially. Virginia worked hard in ladies Auxiliary but felt that some of the member didn't appreciate her methods and decided she would decline if she was elected next year. Virginia took the order to its greatest heights in the community, and her leadership would definitely be missed. Many members hoped to change Virginia's mind, but she decided to return to college, part time, and obtain a degree in business. Darlene Hopkins was elected Worthy Matron and Virginia returned to college. The Order was never the same after Virginia left. Virginia got Cynthia Banner to join the order to bring growth in idealism and support to the chapter.

The time came for the Slaughters to start preparing Carlene for higher education. They started attending the meetings for students who were interested in going to college. One of Carlene's teachers, Ms. Franklin, spoke highly of Carlene's maturity and determination. Virginia and Carlene visited several colleges with Kansas and submitted applications. After visiting all, Carlene chose Fort Hays's State University located in Hays, Kansas.

During that year, Carlene attended her high school prom. This was an adventure for the family, preparing Carlene to attend. Carlos, on the other hand, prepared his "speech of fear" for the young man to take his daughter.

One week prior to prom night, a student brought a gun to school and shot another student in the Junction City High School cafeteria. Carlene and Junior shared this event with their parents. Junior said he was in the cafeteria during the shooting. Carlos and Virginia were glad no one else was harmed. Many parents were upset and wanted actions to be initiated immediately. This incident caused the school to implement police security.

Prom arrived. Virginia was getting Carlene ready for the special evening. Her date was the pastor's son Lee Robertson. Virginia was glad that Lee offered to take Carlene to the prom, but Carlos was still to lecture to the young man. That evening, Carlos invited him to visit the garage for his lecture about hunting and Carlene's curfew time. To ensure the young man will not get any sexual ideas, he also showed the young man his hunting guns. They returned to the house. Virginia and Carlene went upstairs and Lee put on carnation flowers Carlene's wrist, complementing her appearance. Junior rushed upstairs, commented on Lee's suit, and asked to spend the night at Rodney's who lived next door. Virginia and Carlos give their approval. Carlos asked Junior to get his camera from the family room, so he can take pictures of the kids. Carlene kissed her parents goodbye, and Lee escorted her to his car. Carlos yelled again to look at the camera. Carlos walked out, wishing them a good time and mentioned curfew, "Twelve o'clock midnight." The kids drove off waving their hands.

"Carlos, what did you tell that boy? I hope you did not say something to cause them not to have a good time."

"No! I just reminded him how much he needs to be in his best behavior and don't get any ideas that he will regret!"

"I just don't know what to think about you sometimes.

Carlene is a responsible young woman. She's not going to allow anyone to take advantage of her."

"Well, Dear. I'm just making sure that young fellow doesn't get any ideas, even if he's the pastor's son. Now, let's get ready for bed." He escorted Virginia to their bedroom. The next morning, Carlene shared with parents the wonderful time she had, and Lee's determination not to go pass her curfew. Carlene told her mother that he prepared dinner for two at his home. She said that his parents were very nice, and they went to the prom after dinner. Carlene said the dinner was very romantic and she had never met a man who can actually cook. She asked Carlos about his chat with Lee because he was acting a little weird and mentioned his hunting gun. Carlos assured Carlene that they had only casual conversation on hunting and tips on how to kill the beast. Carlos said that he knows exactly what time she should arrive home and his approval of Lee dating her.

One day, at work, Cheryl asked Virginia who her beautician was. Virginia said it's no one special. She went to Barbara Beauty Salon or did it herself. Cheryl invited her to check out Design Creations and gave her a business card. The ladies then discussed their career opportunity and decided it was time for a change. Cheryl transferred to Civilian Personnel Office Center and Virginia transferred to Alcohol and Drugs medical department. Virginia's decision bought sadness to the clinic staff and patients. Virginia's and Cheryl's performance were beyond their duties and they will be missed by the staff and the community.

Virginia loved her new adventure and was amazed about what she learned. Working in a department that was once provided treatment to her marital problems was definitely an adventure. Virginia was exposed to the operational and functional procedures of treating military soldiers who had problems with alcohol and drugs.

The time came for Carlene's greatest moment in her life, graduating from Junction City High School. The Slaughter's home was full with joy, laughter, and sadness. It was time for their first born child to graduate and have a new beginning as a young, intelligent adult. Carlene definitely achieved her goals to make her parents proud.

Virginia and Carlene were busy shopping and preparing for that day. Virginia was also sad because she knew that time was limited, and her daughter will be packing in a few months for college. During that week of preparation, Virginia and Carlene became very close. Carlene shared with her mother her decision on becoming a responsible woman. One of their discussions was financial and birth control. Carlene told her mother that she wanted to use the Norplant for birth control. Carlene said that she wanted to assure that she finish college without the threat of becoming a mother, therefore the Norplant was her best choice. Carlene also shared how she knew that this new start means becoming the woman Virginia desired for her. Virginia was amazed of how Carlene had matured into a woman any mother would be proud of, and that no matter what, she will always be her little girl. Virginia arranged for Carlene to get the Norplant, and, together, the women were ready to face any challenge—vision of change—that waited for them. Financially, Carlene was trained about saving and having a checking account.

The day had arrived. Excited, the Slaughters dressed and went to Carlene's graduation. Carlos, Virginia, and Junior sat waiting for Carlene to come to the stage to receive her diploma and get acknowledged as an honor student. They all yelled and applauded among the crowd when Carlene and Lee walked across the stage. After the graduation ceremony, the family gathered in the parking lot to congratulate Carlene, Sandra, Lee, and the rest of their friends. Carlos had his camera and took pictures of his family and friends to celebrate this great memorable moment. Carlos said its time to go home. Carlene said she will be home later after she takes Sandra home to change clothes. Carlos, Junior, and Virginia arrived home to setup for Virginia's graduation reception party. Virginia pulled out the cake hidden in the guestroom and placed it on the table. Carlos and Junior wanted to cut the cake without Carlene, saying it will be a while before she comes home, and they wanted to eat it already. Virginia said no way, and they can wait for Carlene. Carlene arrived along with her friends. The phone rang and it was grandma Slaughter calling to congratulate Carlene. Carlene received calls from family congratulating her and asking if she received their gifts. Carlene confirmed receipt of gifts from her relatives in Macon, wishing they could be part of their celebration.

After the party, Carlos and Virginia cleaned up the house and settled on the couch in the family room.

"There's going to be a lot of changes ahead for us… our daughter is all grown up now," Carlos said.

"Yep! We have one down and one to go," Virginia said.

"Well, Dear, I know you're going to be bored when Carlene leaves, so I've purchase you a Pekingese puppy. We can pick it up next week, if you still want it."

"Carlos, you're kidding me!"

"No. I'm serious. All we have to do is go pick it up in Olathe. There is a lady who breeds them and has a litter of puppies for sale."

Junior came from his bedroom and entered the family room. "Did I hear you, Dad, that we are getting another dog?"

"Yep. That's if your mom still wants one."

"Mom, say yes!"

"Okay, Junior. Yes, we will get the puppy next week!"

"Now it won't be too boring around here when Carlene leaves. Do you all realize I will have the space downstairs all to myself when Carlene leaves? Man, I can't wait. Oh, Mom, I don't mean that I'm not going to miss Carlene, but finally I have some peace and quiet. Just kidding, Mom!"

Carlos and Virginia kissed Junior good night and went upstairs to their bedroom. The next day, Carlene shared with the family her night on the town and how much fun she had with her friends.

"I can't believe I'm a young woman," said Carlene.

"What do mean, Carlene?" asked Virginia.

"Mom, this is the moment I've been waiting for and now it's finally here."

"I remember how excited I was until I realized what growing up means, no more parents supplying my needs and then I wished I was mama's little girl."

"Mom, you and dad are still going to help me. I'm not getting married. I'm going to school."

"Yes, your dad and I still going to supply some of your needs; but, of course, you are going to have a part-time job, too, because I know you like having your own money and love to buy clothes."

"Oh, yeah, I'm going to check that out as soon as I get to Hays. Who knows they may have Dillions, and I can transfer to their store, but I'm going to check out other jobs. I don't really want to be a cashier."

"All you have to do is pray and God will fill your desires. Now, tell me what Lee's future goals are."

"I think Lee is going into the Air Force. At least that's the last I heard. He's smart enough to go to college, but I don't think he wants to attend. Maybe later or while he's in the Air Force." Carlene was very determined to make her parents proud. Attending college was just the beginning, setting goals to reach her parents' desires for the family.

Fort Hays Picken Hall.

CHAPTER FIVE

THE SLAUGHTERS ADJUST TO CHANGE

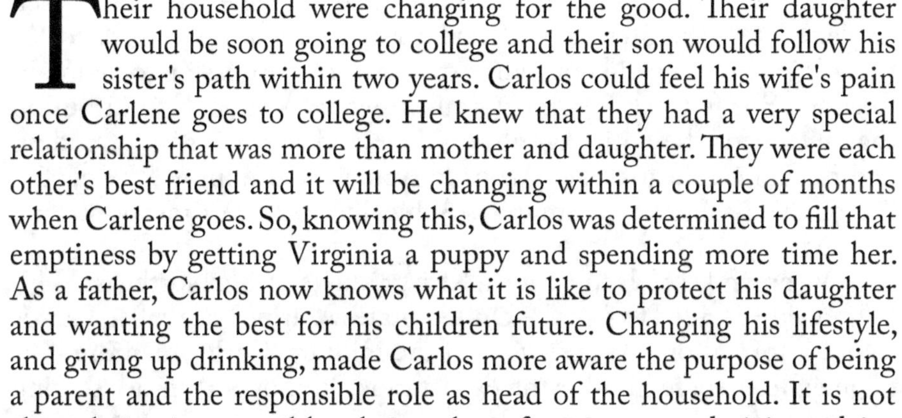

Their household were changing for the good. Their daughter would be soon going to college and their son would follow his sister's path within two years. Carlos could feel his wife's pain once Carlene goes to college. He knew that they had a very special relationship that was more than mother and daughter. They were each other's best friend and it will be changing within a couple of months when Carlene goes. So, knowing this, Carlos was determined to fill that emptiness by getting Virginia a puppy and spending more time her. As a father, Carlos now knows what it is like to protect his daughter and wanting the best for his children future. Changing his lifestyle, and giving up drinking, made Carlos more aware the purpose of being a parent and the responsible role as head of the household. It is not about being in control but being there for support and giving advice for direction in providing guidance for the one you love to make their dreams come true.

The day arrived for the women to attend Carlene's doctor appointment to insert the Noraplant. Carlene admitted that she wanted this procedure done because she knew it will prevent her from getting pregnant for five years and her college attendance was four years. This choice would ensure Carlene to meet her goals without the threat of pregnancy. The women knew that Carlene will explore getting relationships and didn't want to find herself in a situation that would prevent her from reaching her goals. The procedure was successful and now both are comfortable with Carlene attending college and seek her goals.

Carlos and Virginia went to Olathe, Kansas, to pick up the Pekinese puppy. When they arrived to the lady's trailer, they were amazed to see the size of the puppy. The owner, Ms. Woodland loved breeding this type of dog. Carlos and Virginia paid her and left with their puppy. They arrived home, Carlene and Junior were happy to get the puppy. Now they had to name the dog. Virginia decided to let the kids name it. Junior took charge and named the puppy Roc. Everyone agreed and called it Roc. The kids really enjoyed having a puppy, which was surprising to Virginia. She did not expect the kids to take an interest in training it, but they not only trained it, but enjoyed it too.

Carlene and Sandra were now young adults and went out to the clubs in Fort Riley. The girls enjoyed hanging out with their classmates and meeting soldiers, but they both agreed that having a relationship with a soldier was not what their hearts desired. Besides, Carlene believed her father probably would have a fit if she dated a soldier. Carlene knew the lifestyle and career impact the military offered for the soldiers, and she did not want to be a part of the mission to maintain freedom. She felt that her father's enlistment was enough contribution that spoke for the entire family. Carlene had her focus on attending and finishing college with a major to support and improve the quality life of the American community. Achieving her goals meant staying focused.

Meanwhile in Macon, cousin Kirk graduated from Northeast High School. He decided to join the United States Marines. He called Carlos to get information about serving in the military. Carlos mentored his nephew to prepare him for the expectations and opportunities serving in the military. Kirk admired Carlos, his dreams were to see the world through the military. The military also provided financial assistant for soldiers to attend college. Hearing the opportunities Carlene and Junior experienced in the military, Kirk decided he wanted to travel and learn other cultures. The Slaughters was very proud of Kirk's chosen career, wishing him success in fighting for freedom.

The time draw near for Carlene to leave for Fort Hays State University and begin her triumph. The family was busy purchasing the products she would need for her new-found home living in the campus dorms. Virginia and Carlos were proud to have their first born to enter college. But neither of them realized how much it will cost. But the Slaughters managed to provide meet their daughter's needs to set up shelter at the university. They helped pack Carlene's things in Carlos's truck. Then Carlene and Virginia rode in Carlene's car and began their travel to Hays. Carlene was anxious because this as the beginning of her independence from her parents. But her parents ranked among the best role models, so her journey will be successful. As they traveled down I-70, Virginia held back her tears from of thoughts of leaving her little girl at the university. The drive seemed very long and boring, looking at the flat land and seeing nothing but oil field sites. Carlene said that she will leave earlier on Friday when she comes visiting in the weekend.

The Slaughters arrived and went to the Carlene's dorm. They explored the building where Carlene will stay. They liked the building, and thought it was safe, although the rooms were very small. They went out to eat at a restaurant. Carlene said she will miss her mom's cooking. She will have to adjust to restaurants in the area. Hays is a very small town, occupancy depended on the university. Carlene will have the focus she needed to face and complete her chosen challenge. Carlos and Junior said they would not have chosen this institution, but Carlene can adjust to anything. The percentage of black students were seven. Carlene had a challenge and, Carlos had reservations about it, but she says she preferred this environment. Being a military brat was the norm for Carlene. She was used to being among a high percentage of whites and small percentage of blacks. She recalled when her father was station in Okinawa, and she was the only black in her class, but she survived. So, she was sure she will prevail at Fort Hays.

The Slaughters finished their meal and returned Carlene to her dorm to say their good-byes. Carlene cried, wishing her family a safe drive back. "Weekend will be here before we know it, and I will be coming home." Virginia and Carlos held their tears because they did not want to stress her with how much they are going to miss her presence. They encouraged her to be strong. Junior could not wait for Carlene to settle in, and his parents allowed him to spend a weekend on campus. Carlos told him not to forget to us anytime, whether you need anything or not. He also mentioned that the campus sends parent newsletters and that they will be attending the campus events.

The Slaughters arrived at their home in Junction City. The house was never the same that they were less in number. They missed Carlene. Carlos thanked God for this experience, because he remembered how close he came to losing his family due to his drinking, and thanked God for Virginia for allowing him the opportunity explore this adventure as a family. The weekend came, and Carlene would come home frequently.

The Slaughters adjusted to the change and explored family challenging issues.

Junior enjoyed having the downstairs to himself and Roc for companionship. Carlene and Junior would have their disagreement when she came home because she invaded his privacy. But Junior learned to adjust to Carlene weekend visit.

Carlene call home with sadness saying that she did not think she could attend college. She missed being home and was lonely. The academic courses were very challenging and she wanted to quit and come home. Virginia listened at Carlene's depression on the phone and told her daughter that she can return home any time she wants. She reminded Carlene that the only employment that she would probably qualify for was returning to Dillons, Burger King, or McDonalds due to lack of experience and education. Once Virginia drew the vision of change, Carlene would choose for herself if she decides not to finish college. Carlene had a change of heart. She called Virginia that same week and said she was doing fine and decided to hang in there. Carlene said that she was just depressed and thanked her Mom for reminding her why she chose to attend college. Carlene thought her mother would open her arms and say that she would take care of Carlene's needs and desires, but Virginia reminded her daughter what she would have to face the challenges of employment to provide her own. Virginia's reluctance to embrace her daughter's fear of failure bought greater encouragement and a chance to be successful.

Carlene became very successful at Fort Hays State University. She finally reached out and embraced friendship among the students and staff. Her weekend visits vanished and evolved into monthly then holiday visitation. Carlos asked Virginia about not seeing or hearing from Carlene often, and Virginia would reply, "Our daughter has finally faced the challenges of life and learn the lesson of independence."

Virginia and Carlos became focused on Junior ensuring that he maintain his grades and supporting his participation in sports. Junior was great in basketball and baseball, making the *Daily Union* headlines.

Carlos confronted Virginia about getting Roc neutered. Virginia agreed and Carlos made the arrangement with their veterinarian. The procedure was not a success. The vet administered too much anesthesia to Roc, which caused the puppy to go blind. Carlos and Virginia were devastated of the results. Carlos took Roc to a specialist at K-state, hoping for a resolution to treat Roc, but they only confirmed what caused the puppy's blindness. Therefore, Carlos decided to press charges again the Veterinarian Clinic facility. The Veterinarian didn't charge Carlos for the procedure in hope that Carlos would drop the case, insisting that the procedures were not the cause of Roc's blindness. The trial was held and veterinarian were surprised to see Roc presented to judge his illness as a result of the procedure. Carlos won the case and Roc was put to sleep.

Carlos knew Virginia would be hurt with their decision. The family had grown to love Roc as a family member who brought happiness and comfort. Carlos he immediately put away all of Roc's belongings to diminish Virginia's pain. Roc was more than a puppy but was treated as a human being who had a purpose in life and was taken away. The Slaughters did not get another pet.

It was time for the Annual Job Fair held at Fort Riley. Virginia's supervisor granted her time off to attend the fair to participate in the giveaway vacation trip. Virginia didn't want to attend, but her colleague persuaded her to change her mind. Virginia attended the job fair and won a family roundtrip to Orlando, Florida. The drawings were held the day of the event and Virginia was notified as the winner. Virginia's colleagues congratulated her of her winnings. Virginia immediately called Carlos at work to share the news and Carlos didn't believe Virginia until he saw the winner's vacation trip package. The Slaughters were excited sharing their winnings with Junior. Junior was very happy for his mother, but decided not to go to Orlando, Florida.

Virginia and Carlos went to Orlando and left Junior with Carlene who was on fall break. Carlos and Virginia had a wonderful time. This was the honeymoon vacation they never experienced. They toured the grounds of Orlando Universal Studios, Sea World, and Magic Kingdom and visited more adventure parks. Carlos and Virginia had the time of their lives relaxing and enjoying the adventures of Orlando. The time had arrived for the couple to depart Florida, a vacation they will treasure.

Carlos and Virginia returned to Junction City. They shared their trip with family and friends, showing pictures Carlos took. They both decided that this was the beginning of a new adventure they would include more trips in their marriage and enjoy the fun of exploring the wonderful sites throughout the United States. Planning vacation trips adds sparks and relaxing, romantic adventures that rejuvenates the marriage relationship.

Carlene was very happy for her parents. She and Junior saw the romantic sparks in their relationship. Carlene returned to college, sharing with her classmates her parents' adventure. Mr. Cottingham would call Carlene periodically and Carlene shared parents' trip. Mr. Cottingham was pleased to hear that his daughter and family were very happy.

Mr. Cottingham would call Carlene and not get a response.

He often left messages and became concerned, so he called Virginia and mentioned his calls to Carlene absence. Virginia called Carlene and mentioned that her grandfather called with concerns because she would not be in her room when he called. Carlene told her mother that she would be out eating dinner or visiting her classmates during the time her grandfather would call. Carlene also mentioned that she was dating and would like bringing her friend home to meet the family. Virginia agreed for Carlene to invite her friend to visit. Virginia told Carlos and Junior and they were not excited to hear the news. In fact, they both said they would have to give their approval for Carlene to continue to date this guy. Virginia shook her head and smiled saying, "I hope Carlene and her boyfriend are prepared for her family interview session."

Carlene and Kevin arrived at the Slaughter home on a weekend visit. They extended their welcome and Junior escorted Kevin to the guest room reminding him not to get any ideas about visiting Carlene's bedroom. That room is off limits. You only can visit with Carlene in the family room, kitchen and living room. Kevin smiled and entered the guestroom to unpack. Kevin and Carlene were in the family room, waiting for the Slaughters to joined them and interview Kevin. Carlos, Virginia, and Junior presented their questions and Carlos invited Kevin to his palace the garage where he enjoys fixing his vehicle, storing his hunting gear and tools. Kevin was amazed to see Carlos's tool collections. The men chatted about their hobbies and found they had something in common. Virginia and Carlos were pleased with Kevin.

"So, Mom, what do you think of my boyfriend?"

"He seems to be very nice and have good manners."

"Mom, we are just friends… nothing serious."

"Well, I'm glad to hear that and to know that you have found you someone to love."

"Mom, I'm not sure if I'm in love, but I do know that I enjoy our friendship."

"That's enough for now. If you all get serious, I'm sure you will let me know."

Carlene and Kevin's visit was a success. They enjoyed Kevin's visit and invited him to come again. Kevin assured Carlene's parents that he will be back to visit. Kevin told Carlene that her parents are nice and her mother looked very young for her age. Kevin knew then how Carlene will look at that age since she had her mothers' features. They packed her Carlene's car and returned to Fort Hays. Carlene would often bring classmates periodically to visit during the weekend or holidays. Carlos and Virginia would visit Fort Hays to support their events. Carlene was in a musical opera. They were very surprised that Carlene was singing in the opera. Carlos and Virginia were not fans of musicals but attended the event to support her. They enjoyed the musical and were proud of Carlene. Junior told her that the only reason he came was because she was his sister, but this is definitely not his cup of tea. The family stayed overnight and hung out with Carlene and her friends. The family finally got the opportunity to meet Dr. Marianne Horton who was an activist for African-American heritage. She invited the family to attend their homecoming parade the next day. Virginia's road the float and Carlos and Junior stood on the sidelines taking pictures hanging out with Carlene colleague who were not in the Parade. Virginia enjoyed this event sharing and exploring Carlene adventure attending FHSU. The parade ended and Virginia, Dr. Horton, and Carlene found Carlos and Junior among the crowd. Dr. Horton thanked the Slaughters for coming to their weekend events. She said that Carlene definitely has a lovely family and that she enjoys being a motherly role model for Carlene.

"Carlene is a student you want to support. She knows what she wants in life and works hard toward her goal. That's why I'm mentoring Carlene. I'm going to see to it that Carlene is very successful in whatever she chooses to do. She's the image of a daughter I never had," Dr. Horton said.

"Thanks, Dr. Horton for that lovely comment. My daughter definitely has mentioned your name many of times, and I'm glad that she has a mentor like you!" said Virginia.

"Are you all staying for the game tonight?

"No, I have to get back due to duty call," said Carlos. "But I'm glad we came to see Carlene sing opera."

"I do understand and thanks again for your support."

The Slaughters waved good-bye to Dr. Horton and jumped in Virginia's car and returned to their hotel. Kevin drove his car and told he will meet them at the hotel. The Slaughters packed and ate dinner with Carlene and Kevin and departed for Junction City.

Once the Slaughters arrived in Junction City, Carlos reported to the unit to prepare for the restructure of units at Fort Riley. Carlos will be assigned to 1/5 Field Artillery due to the Big Red One returning to Germany during this year 1995.

The First Infantry Division, more commonly known as the "Big Red One," or the "Fighting First," came to Fort Riley from Germany in 1955 and remained in Kansas until 1995. Now, Fort Riley is known as Home of America's Army. Carlos transition change was due to the restructure of Fort Riley change to Home of America's Army. In early 1996, as part of the reorganization of the Army, the 1st Infantry Division was demobilized at Fort Riley and reactivated at Würzburg, Germany. Two brigades of the Big Red One are stationed in Germany, along with the Division headquarters and support elements, and one brigade is stationed at Ft. Riley, Kansas. The Division reestablished an army museum for the Big Red One in Würzburg and the First Division Museum at Cantigny continued to support both the Fort Riley and Würzburg museum activities.

One day, Carlos arrived at home from work and presented Virginia with an invitation to attend a dining out formal unit event to be held at the Riley Restaurant. Virginia was excited. The phone rang. It was Virginia's mom informing her that her cousin Jermaine had been arrested for murder.

"How can this happen?" Virginia asked.

"Well, they said that the guy and Jermaine were auguring and Jermaine pulled out his gun and shot him. We spoke with Jermaine, and he said the guy entered his apartment, uninvited threatening him and he shot him in fear that the guy had a gun. But the guy was not armed."

"Mom... I hate to hear Jermaine was arrested.

Are you alright?"

"Yep, I'm doing fine. I just was having pain in my legs. Tricia is going to take me to the doctor tomorrow. I will call you with the results."

Moments later, the phone rang again, it was Mr. Scott from the publishing company announcing that they received feedback to advised Virginia to wait until they have a better publishing deal. They also told Virginia they will send copies of the publisher company's response.

Virginia called her girlfriend Cheryl to get the number to her beautician Design Creations. Virginia scheduled an appoint with Pamela. Virginia arrived to her scheduled appointment and was shocked. It was very nice and clean. She seated herself and waited patiently. While waiting for Pamela to finish with her client, Virginia overheard military spouses discussing going out to the club getting their grove on at the VFW. The women were also discussing marital problems and how they couldn't wait to leave Fort Riley. There was one lady who apparently loved telling jokes. She was very funny and all the women suggested that she become a comedian. Pamela said that Marcy always telling jokes.

"One day Marcy is going to say the wrong this to the wrong person and get her feelings hurt!" said Pamela.

"Girl, I don't think I'm going to get my feelings hurt for telling the true. I'm serious. The young mothers need to get their lives straight. As soon as their husbands go the field or NTC, they get restless and go to the club to find Joe Blow. Some of them even get pregnant by Joe Blow and say it's their husband's child. You know I know because I like to go out and relax, but I go with my husband and I see these women who come up in here to get their hair done, in the club and it's not their spouse. Now, that's wrong and they say that I'm going to get my feelings hurt. I don't think so."

"Virginia, you can come and sit in my chair. I'm sorry you had to wait, but I'm just a little bit behind," said Pamela.

"That's okay," Virginia replied.

"Hey, I know you... I always attend the Eastern Star events. They haven't sponsored an event in a while. What's going on?" Marcy asked.

"Oh! I don't know, they have a new Worthy Matron. I'm not serving that officer seat anymore."

"Well, they need to get busy. I thought something had changed, because I haven't heard anything about sponsoring Fashion Shows or Dances. Girl, you need to go back in the seat, because they aren't doing anything now."

"Well, I'm busy going to school now, and I don't have the time, but I do attend some meetings."

"Well... I just want you to know that you had it going on and let me know when y'all are going to be sponsoring events again, because I just love coming to y'all event. I heard that they are still sponsoring some events, but not that many people come out. What are they doing?"

"I have no idea!"

"Pamela, how much I owe you? I'm fixing to go. It was nice chatting with you Virginia."

Pamela wrote a check for payment of services. Pamela and Virginia said good-bye to Marcy. Pamela apologized for Marcy's behavior. Virginia replied saying no apology is necessary. Pamela washes and sets Virginia's hair. Virginia loved Pamela's work and scheduled her next appointment.

That evening, Virginia and Carlos got dress and went to the dining out at Riley Restaurant. Just as Carlos was getting ready to leave the house, Carlos asked Junior his opinion or how he looks. Junior said that both of his parents look good and tease them with their own statement. "Don't forget your curfew."

When they arrived at Riley's, Carlos asked Virginia what she's drinking and she asked for a glass of wine and Carlos got himself a coke. Carlos brought Virginia her glass of wine and comment how radiant she looks, saying that he couldn't wait until the night is over and kissed Virginia. Carlos's commander joined Virginia at their table and Carlos introduced his wife. The Commander was glad they decided to come out and Virginia replied that she was having a great time and they should do this more often. Carlos walked around taking pictures and dancing with Virginia periodically. The couple had a wonderful time mingling with Carlos's colleagues. The couple left the event and returned home making passionate love all night long.

CHAPTER SIX

NIGHTMARE TRAGEDY

Months later, Carlos unit was preparing for NTC. Carlos again was preparing to leave his family to attend the unit annual training exercise. Carlos was getting tired of leaving his family and decided that when he became eligible, he would retire. Carlos also became eligible for promotion to Sergeant First Class. The news of Carlos promotion was a celebration for the family. Virginia coordinated a surprise party inviting all of Carlos's friend and soldiers to the event at their home. Virginia arranged for Leon to get Slaughter out of the house so Virginia and Rosetta could prepare for the party. Leon barbequed the meat, and Virginia and Rosetta prepared the side dishes. The ladies, friends, and soldier began to gather at the Slaughter's home preparing for the celebration feast. Junior announced that Leon and Carlos were pulling into the driveway. Family, friends, and soldiers gathered downstairs waiting for Carlos to enter. Carlos and Leon entered the Slaughters home and Virginia and Rosetta told Leon to change the music downstairs. Carlos and Leon went downstairs and the ladies followed behind them and Carlos's friends, soldiers, and family all yelled, "Surprise!" Carlos was shocked and had no idea what was going on until this moment. Leon mentioned how difficult it was for him to keep Slaughter away. Everyone mentioned their part in surprising Carlos, and he thanked his wife, family, and friends for organizing this event. Carlos quietly walked through the crowd and embraces Virginia, declaring his love and thanks. Mr. Cottingham called wishing Carlos congratulations, saying that he didn't want to hear no conversation about Carlos getting out of the military. Carlos thanked Mr. Cottingham and returned the phone to Virginia. Virginia told her father how Carlos reacted and hung up the phone. Virginia joins the party admiring Carlos relaxing and enjoining family and friends.

Weeks later, Carlos went to NTC. He constantly called his family informing them of his adventure and while listening to their conversation how much he's missed. Junior states how he's the man of house and how he's taking good care of Virginia. Carlos mentioned that one of his soldiers was injured during an exercise. Apparently, one of the soldiers from another unit 101st Infantry had an accident while delivering supplies. The soldier broke his leg and injured his back during a training exercise enemy attack. Virginia was sad to hear the news and advised Carlos to be careful. Carlos assured Virginia that will apply safety in all exercises he must perform.

A month later, Carlos returned home, Virginia and Junior greeted him at the unit. Carlene was in college and couldn't attend the unit welcome home troops celebrations. The Slaughters left the unit celebrations and returned home. They pulled into the driveway and entered the house and Carlene surprised her family. Virginia and Carlos were very surprised, but Junior was aware of Carlene coming home. Carlos was excited and happy because everyone was home to greet his return.

A month later, Virginia decided that she wanted to change her career and applied for Military Personnel. She told Cheryl that personnel was her heart's desires, therefore, Virginia submitted her application. Weeks later, Virginia received a call from Tricia saying that Ms. Cottingham was ill. Virginia immediately told the family and arranged for her flight. Carlos took his wife to the Kansas City, Missouri airport. They arrived at the airport and Carlos and Junior waited until his wife boarded the plane. Carlos comforted Virginia saying that her mother will be okay. Virginia had doubts about her mother's illness, but kissed Carlos saying how much she loves him and embrace and kiss Junior to take care of his father and board the plane. Junior and Carlos returned to the car and departed for Junction City, Kansas.

Virginia arrived at Atlanta airport. Tricia, Shawn, and Bro greeted Virginia when she came through the passenger's arrival entry. Virginia hugged and kissed everyone and they all went to the baggage claim to retrieve Virginia's luggage. They loaded Bro's vehicle and departed for Macon. While traveling to Macon from the airport, Tricia informed Virginia of Mrs. Cottingham conditions.

They arrived to Mrs. Cottingham home. Virginia went to her grandmother's bedroom to visit.

"Hey there, Virginia, how was your trip? My girl is still looking good. Come and sit down," Grandma said.

Virginia sat down with grandma and heard the updated news concerning her mother's illness. She told Virginia that apparently Mrs. Cottingham diabetes is causing her illness. The doctors had admitted Mrs. Cottingham in the hospital because she had lost activity in her legs and the doctors were running tests to find out what the problem was. Tricia and Shawn joined them in grandma's bedroom after putting away Virginia's luggage in her old bedroom. Virginia's phones Carlos to let him know she has arrived, providing him with the updated news. Hours later, Tricia and Shawn took Virginia to the hospital to see Mrs. Cottingham. Mrs. Cottingham was so glad to see her daughter. Virginia went to her mother's beside with sadness in her eyes. She encouraged her mother to have faith that everything will be alright, wiping the tears from her mother eyes. Her mother smiled and said how glad she was to see her daughter. Mrs. Cottingham asked Virginia on how her family was doing and did them come with her. Virginia told her mother that her family couldn't join her on this trip.

Meanwhile in Junction City, Carlos and Junior were going through some difficult times. Carlos was not pleased with Junior's change of attitude. Carlos suspected his son has an interest in dating girls and gave him a lecture about sex. Junior informed Carlos that he already knew about being sexually active and about relationships, insisting that he had no interest, but Carlos presented his son with a box of condoms for his protection, if the moment occurred. In Georgia, Virginia, and Tricia visited her father who is doing fine. He asked Virginia about her mother's illness. Virginia updated her father with the latest news. Mr. Cottingham said that he hadn't gone to the hospital but intended to visit her mother tomorrow. Hours later, Virginia ended her visit with her father and Virginia and Tricia went to the hospital to visit her mother.

At the hospital, the doctor told Virginia about her mother's illness, saying how important it was for her mother to follow her diet concerning her diabetes and blood pressure. The doctor also mentioned a possible large cyst located in her mother's uterus, but they cannot perform surgery at this time. The doctor assured Virginia that her mother's condition can be treated, but she must stay in the hospital for a while. Virginia went to see her mother encouraging Mrs. Cottingham that everything is going to be alright and once her mother is release they will arrange for a nurse to care for her during the day until Tricia came home from work. Virginia called Carlos and told Carlos of her arriving date and time. Virginia sensed something is wrong by the tone of Carlos's voice, but Carlos assured his wife that everything is fine, and not to worry because he has everything under control.

Carlos told Junior of his mother's call when he returned from baseball practice. He also asked Junior if he wanted to go with him to the airport to pick up Virginia. Junior said that he had an English test and couldn't miss his class. Therefore, Carlos will go to Kansas City to pick up Virginia and told Junior that after baseball practice to come straight home.

Junior is having problems with peer pressure. He's experiencing being a popular student among his fans of sports. He has to face the pressure of hanging out with the wrong crowd who indulged in alcohol and drugs. After practice, Junior arrived home and there was a knock at the door. It's Randolph, Junior's next-door friend and neighbor. Randolph needed to talk with Junior and wanted to come in. Junior allowed Randolph to enter and they went downstairs. Randolph asked Junior when his mother is coming home. Junior informed Randolph that his dad had gone to pick up his mother from the airport. The boys chatted and Junior discovered that Randolph had experienced drugs and he invited Junior to join him. Randolph said that his parents were having financial problems and neglected him and his brother, therefore, his only comfort was drugs. Junior informed Randolph that he wanted nothing to do with drugs. Randolph accepted Junior's response and left saying, "You will try it either now or later." Randolph left, dropping the unfinished small piece of marijuana on the family room floor.

Meanwhile in Georgia, Tricia takes Virginia to the Atlanta airport. Virginia went to the boarding entry informing Tricia to call her, waving good-bye. Tricia waved good-bye to Virginia, yelling that she will call her to update her about Mrs. Cottingham's condition. Tricia left the airport and drove back to Macon.

Virginia arrived at the airport and walked through the arrival entry and saw Carlos waiting. Carlos walked and embraced Virginia with a kiss, taking her carry-on luggage and they went to the baggage claim section to pick up Virginia's luggage and departed for Junction City. They arrived home and Junior came from downstairs, embracing his mother with a hug and kiss saying how much he missed her and helped his dad with the luggage. Virginia changed her clothes. Meanwhile,

Carlos went downstairs and noticed the balcony door was unlocked, but he also saw a piece of marijuana roach located on the floor. He picked up the marijuana roach and examined it, wondering if Junior was using drugs. But wasn't Junior's, it belonged to Randolph who dropped it as he was leaving their home after visiting Junior. Carlos locked the door and went upstairs to put away the evidence. He decided not to mention it to Virginia due to her plate being full with worries of her mother's illness.

Within a few weeks, Virginia noticed Carlos's behavior towards Junior, mentioning to Carlos not to be so hard on Junior. Virginia noticed that Junior was receiving a lot of calls from his friends and implemented a certain time allowed for Junior to receive calls and after that time, no called from his friends due to Junior needing plenty of rest to get up in the mornings to attend school. Virginia also told Junior that she noticed he was receiving calls from this particular girl and had a conversation with Junior about sex. Junior informed Virginia that Carlos had spoken with him about sex and said that he's not interested in sex.

"I've already had this conversation with dad when you went to Georgia. Man, why are y'all beating this? Do you want me to be gay?"

"No. That's not why we are discussing sex with you. We just don't want you to get into a situation that will affect you for the rest of life, being a parent before you are ready.

"Mom, I know about sex and using condoms.

Dad and I have already discussed this and he bought me some condoms expressing that he was not giving me permission to have sex, but just as you say, if the moment arrived, use a condom."

"Did he tell you not to believe it when a girl tells you that she's taking birth control pills or using some type of birth control method to keep from getting pregnant?"

"Mom, dad said enough and I'm not going to get some girl pregnant. Okay?"

Virginia was glad to hear from Junior that Carlos had spoken to Junior. When Carlos arrived home, Virginia mentioned her confrontation with Junior and what she discovered. Carlos told Virginia that he didn't want to discuss this with her because she was all wrapped up with her mother's illness and she appeared to be stressed out enough, but since she's aware that Junior was at that age and may have an interest in sex, they must have a family discussion.

"Junior doesn't want to have any more discussions about sex," Virginia said.

"Junior is not grown and will not tell me when not to discuss anything in this house. Now, we are going to have a conversation with him tonight."

Carlos and Virginia arranged to have a family discussion with Junior about peer pressure, dating, and sex. Carlos addressed the issue of using drugs and Junior denied using or having the desires. Virginia noticed Carlos's approach discussing drugs and sensed that Carlos may think that Junior was using. After their family discussion, Virginia continued to discuss this issue in their bedroom while Junior was outside in the garage. Carlos told Virginia that Junior was a teenager and sometimes, due to peer pressure, will use drugs. Virginia asked Carlos if he was saying that Junior used drugs. Carlos replied that he doesn't know but noticed Junior's grades have dropped. Virginia reminded Carlos that Junior's grades dropped a little when he was active in sports and that was why she had implemented Junior not to receive calls after a certain time so he can focus on doing his homework and study for tests. Carlos ended their conversation and still did not mention the marijuana he found downstairs when he went to pick up Virginia at the airport. The thought that Carlos may suspect Junior of using drugs troubled Virginia.

Virginia received a call from Tricia saying that Mr. Cottingham was rushed to the hospital as he was experiencing severe stomach pain. She said that Mr. Cottingham's condition was not good. The doctors didn't think he's going to survive this surgery. Virginia informs Tricia that she will be taking the next plane out. Virginia informed Carlos and Junior about Mr. Cottingham and called the airlines to book a flight to Atlanta.

The next day, Carlos took Virginia to the airport. Carlos saw the fear in Virginia's eyes, wishing that everything went well with her father's illness. Virginia boarded the plane and waved good-bye to Carlos.

Virginia arrived at the Atlanta airport and exited the arrival entrance. Tricia and her boyfriend, Walt, greeted Virginia, and they went to the baggage claim to retrieve her luggage.

"How was the flight?" Walt asked. "It seemed like it was yesterday you left and now you're back again. I told Tricia I know y'all will be glad when these sicknesses end."

"The flight was okay. I just wanted to thank you for supporting my sister during this difficult time in our life. What is going on with our parents? I was just here a few months ago to see mother and now it's dad. I don't know how much more I can take. I'm sorry you and

I have not had much conversation. You are always there at the family gathering, but we never get the opportunity to chat."

"You don't have to apologize. I know when you and Tricia get together, there is no Walt and Tricia time and I understand because you don't live here and y'all try to play catch up. I've learned to be just like Carlos to give Tricia space when her sister in town."

"You are right... I'm glad you understand sisterhood."

"Walt knows how we are when we get together," Tricia said. "I started not to call, but when the doctor mentioned this is serious and dad may not recover from this surgery, I decided to call."

"How is mother doing?"

"She's fine and glad when I told her you were coming home. I haven't told mom that the doctors don't think dad is going to make it.

"Good... because mom doesn't need to be worried."

Virginia arrived in Macon and visited family and friend along with spending time at the hospital with her father. Mr. Cottingham's health is improving and the doctors decided to transfer him to the Rehabilitation Center to recover because he needed professional health care. The doctor told Virginia that she can return home indicating that Mr. Cottingham's recovery will be a success. Virginia visited Mrs. Slaughter to apologize for not visiting her when she was in Macon due to her mother's illness. Mrs. Slaughter understood and asked Virginia about her father's illness. Virginia provided Mrs. Slaughter with the updated information about her father's illness saying that he will be returning home tomorrow.

Virginia chatted with her mother's nurse and discovered that her mother is doing fine with home care treatment. Virginia saw that Tricia is doing a great job assisting the nurse and hated that she was so far away during her parents' illness. Both of Virginia's parents appreciated their daughter's concerns and stated that they are proud that Virginia has a family and not to worry about them.

Virginia, Tricia, and Walt went to the hospital for the last time to see Mr. Cottingham before Tricia took Virginia to the airport. He questioned them about the whereabouts Tricia's friend. Virginia told him that he's waiting outside in the hallway. "Tell him to come inside the room," Mr. Cottingham said. "I'm glad that Tricia left that other guy alone because he had a weird personality." Walt came into the room and said hello saying he will be back to pick up the girls. Mr. Cottingham was in a weird spirit. He was glad to see the girls but discussed all his failure in life revealing his relationship with his brother, marital infidelity, and he wished he could have accomplished raising his children. Virginia and Tricia were listening in shock because they knew their father would have never declared his life story with them. The girls assumed it was the medication and made a vow to each other to mention the topic again when their father recovers.

Tricia and Virginia departed the hospital and drove to the Atlanta airport. Virginia phoned Carlos once she arrived to ensure that he will meet her at Kansas airport. Virginia boarded the plane waving goodbye to Tricia.

When Virginia arrived home, Junior had some exciting news. He passed the drivers' test. Virginia was very proud of Junior. The phone rang. It was Cheryl requesting to speak with Virginia. Cheryl and Virginia discuss her trip to Georgia and their husbands' upcoming assignments. They discussed how they wanted to stay in the area until their children graduate and more.

"Yell, Mom... now I can drive your car to school."

"I don't think so... you will still ride the bus. Now, I will allow you to drive sometimes to your afternoon sport practice.

"Mom, now you and dad can get me a car."

"Junior, you will get a car when you save your money to help buy it."

"Okay. Mom, this summer I'm going to get me a job and miss basketball camp."

"Junior, that's your decision. I just told you what my requirements and expectations were of you. It is up to you to meet our requirements."

"Okay, Mom... I got it. Give me a kiss!"

Junior rushed down the stairs and out the door. Carlos seemed to be worried about something, and Virginia question him about his behavior.

"Virginia, I called DA to check on the status of my next assignment and it is not good news."

"What do you mean it's not good news?"

"Well, Dear... it seems that they need my MOS in Korea and I don't want to go to Korea. Well, I'm not going. It's as simple as that, but I'm working with someone who may be able to get my assignment changed. I told them of my family situation, but as we know that don't mean anything. But I'm going to give it a shot and see if I can stay here, especially since Carlene is in college and Junior will be graduating next year."

"Well, dear... I knew our number was coming up. Cheryl and I spoke the other day about our husband's coming up for assignment.

You know I will not leave Carlene out here by herself, so I hope you can do something."

Three days have passed and Virginia is back to work. It's a busy day for the clinic. They have a lot of soldier's enrolled in the program and the counselors are pulling their hair out waiting for the day to end. Carolyn, a counselor, entered Virginia's office to chat.

"Girl, it has been so crazy around here and I forgot to ask you how your father is doing. Is everything okay?"

"He's doing fine. Matter of fact, I was just getting ready to call the hospital to check on him." Virginia's phone rang.

"Hello. May I please speak with Mrs. Slaughter?" the nurse asked.

"This is Mrs. Slaughter. How may I help you?"

"Mrs. Slaughter, this is the Rehabilitation Center. Your father's condition has changed. He has pneumonia, and we don't expect him to make it through the night. He asked me to call you. Hold on while I give him the phone."

"Hello, Dad... what wrong?" Virginia was tears.

"Gina... dad is not feeling good." Mr. Cottingham struggled to speak.

"Dad, now you got to hang in there. Don't you leave me... Dad, do you hear me? Don't you leave me. Dad... I love you, please just hang in there. You must fight, don't give up. Please, Dad... I love you."

"Gina, I love you, too." He grasped for air.

The nurse removes the phone from Mr. Cottingham's hand. "Mrs. Slaughter, your father is very weak and we don't expect him to make it through the night. So, I'm calling you per his request. I'm going to have to hang up now to assist the nurses to care for your father." She hung up the phone.

"Carolyn, my daddy is not going to make it. He's dying."

Carolyn embraced Virginia and wiping her eyes with tissue from Virginia desk. "Come on, Virginia. Now you got to be strong for your father. What did the nurse say?"

"The nurse said they don't expect my daddy to make it through the night."

"Virginia, get your things. You need to go home and see about getting a flight out of here. I'll let your supervisor know what's going on.

"Thanks, Carolyn!"

"Are you sure that you are okay and can drive home?"

"Yep, I'm sure... I need to go home... bye!"

Virginia drove home and called Carlos at work to inform him of her father's condition. Carlos hung up and said he is on his way home. Carlos told his commander that his spouse's father is dying and requested emergency leave. Carlos arrived home and found his wife in tears lying on the bed.

"Virginia!"

Virginia Rise up from lying down on the bed in tears) Carlos my Dad is dying, I got to go home!"

Carlos sat on the bed, hugging his wife and wiping her tears. Honey. Everything is going to be okay. What did the nurse say?"

Virginia told Carlos on the latest news in reference to her father's illness. The Slaughters prepared for travel. Junior came home from school and was told that they will be going home. Virginia called Carlene to inform her that grandpa was dying. Carlene said that she will pack and was on her way home that night. Virginia lectured Carlene not to drive and wait until morning. They will leave once she arrived. Virginia called Tricia and Tricia said that she just left the hospital and Mr. Cottingham was on a respiratory. They didn't expect him to live through the night.

Early the next morning, around 3 a.m., Virginia received a call. It was Tricia crying saying that Mr. Cottingham has died. Virginia put the phone down, in tears saying, "He's gone. My father is dead."

Carlos grabbed the phone from Virginia hands. Carlos spoke to Tricia who was crying. Calm down, Tricia. I'm going to hang up and we are on our way!"

Carlene arrives home around 9 a.m. and the Slaughters loaded up Virginia's car with their luggage and droves to Macon. They arrive in Macon late that night. The family gathered at Mr. Cottingham's home to make funeral arrangements. Carlos was giving his support to Virginia, not leaving for one moment giving, his assistance as needed. Mr. Cottingham's brother, Ted, Lisa's nieces and nephews came over to provide their assistance among other family members. Tricia and Virginia silently left their guests and went to Mr. Cottingham's bedroom and went through his files.

"Virginia, I was just thinking after looking at this doctor's appointments. Daddy must have known that he probably would not survived this illness if his intestines ruptured. Read this doctor report," said Tricia.

"Yep, I agree... he must have had a spiritual feeling about his death. Tricia looked at the date this was written. That's during the time daddy was discussing with us about his Life Insurance. I just realized that's why daddy revealed his passed life experiences with us, because he knew he was not going to survive.

"Yep, because he would have never discussed his personal life experience with us, and we thought we would have the opportunity to tease him."

"I should have never left. I should have stayed."

"No, Gina, you did the right thing. We based our decision on the doctor recovery information and dad would not have wanted you to be here without your family. You know how he was when it came to you and your family. At least you got the chance to see him before he died."

Ted and Lisa entered the bedroom. Ted said, "What are y'all doing?"

"We just were reminiscing over the pass of daddy's last days. I'm going to miss him."

"Yep, my brother had his ways and I just hate that we didn't have a loving relationship as brothers. We all are going to miss him. Did y'all let the funeral director know that my brother served in United States Army?"

"Yep, that's already taken cared of.

"Now, y'all got to stop all that crying," Lisa said.

"Here, Tricia... wipe your eyes."

"You are right... I need to save my tears, because I know I'm going to breakdown at the funeral. Virginia and I have done the eulogy."

"We all are going to breakdown."

"John, your daddy's best friend wants to be on the program for special remarks," Lisa said. "John also said that your father wanted his civilian pins on his blue suit."

"Okay... that's fine. Dad told us about his chosen suit and his civilian pins, which I found on the dresser. It's as if my father knew this day was coming soon."

The ladies and Ted left the bedroom and returned to their guests. All their family and friends mingled together, reminiscing Mr. Cottingham's last days of life.

That Saturday afternoon, the family gathered at Mr. Cottingham's home for funeral assembly and droves to Killeen, Georgia, to Mt. Calvary for the funeral ceremony. Mr. Cottingham was buried at the church cemetery as he requested. The church was full with standing room only. Mr. Cottingham was a popular and well-known individual. Many of his friends didn't know that he had children. Mr. Cottingham's close friends presented their remarks of their fallen friend and colleague. At the graveside, Virginia was presented with the United States Army flag as the soldiers played the "Taps," lowering the casket in the ground. Mr. Cottingham had joined his deceased family member at the church cemetery.

Days later, Carlos and Virginia settled her father's estate splitting his belonging among his children and family members. The girls decided to wait to tell Mrs. Cottingham due to her illness. Virginia and her family departed Macon in sadness saying good-bye to a man well known and loved.

Virginia was very distraught over the death of her father. When they returned home, Carlene did everything she could to keep her mother busy.

But one week later, Virginia decided it was time to go through her father's things that she brought back from Georgia. Virginia opened the box in her bedroom with Mr. Cottingham's photos. Virginia opened the envelope with the photos and was surprised when she saw photos of herself when she was a toddler. Carlene entered the bedroom and sees her mother looking at the photos. Virginia told Carlene that she hadn't seen the photos in years. The last time Virginia can recall seeing these photos were when her mother and father lived in South Macon. Virginia thought the picture had been destroyed accidentally but, all this time, her father had them. There were also pictures of Mr. Cottingham when he was stationed in Korea. Tears began to run down Virginia's face as she tells Carlene how much she's going to miss her father.

"I have missed a lot of time over the years of my parent's life. I wished that my life could have been different and I could have shared special occasions with my parents before they aged."

"Mom, your parents understood that your life was with being with dad and us. It's good to cry, you need to get it out of your system. There is nothing wrong with crying."

"I'm sorry, Carlene, but it just hurt so bad."

"I know. Mom, it will get better. I don't know what I would do if anything happened to you and dad. I don't think I'll be as strong as you are right now."

"The only thing that's keeping me going now is my family."

Virginia found photos of her father and she put her father's photo and her childhood pictures in a frame and placed them in the family room. Virginia will never be the same, but she will learn how to accept this loss and move forward through life as she explores the vision of change. Carlene returned to Fort Hays State University, and the family learned how to accept Virginia's new emotional grief, the loss of one of her greatest love one.

Prom night was approaching for Junior's junior year at Junction City High School. Carlos and Junior went to pick out his rental tuxedo from Tom's Men Wear and Virginia purchased wrist floral for Junior's date. Virginia was shock that Junior's date was a black girl Tasha. Junior head was spinning the closer prom night was approaching. He asked Virginia can he use her car. Virginia approved Junior to use her car.

Prom night had arrived and Carlos brought out the camera. His attitude was different for Junior's prom night than it was with Carlene. Carlene arrive home from Hays just in time to see her brother preparing to leave. Carlos took pictures of Junior's Randolph tuxedo dress attire. The attire was elegant. Carlene waited for Carlos to tell Junior what time he should return home. Carlos didn't mention a time, and Carlene set the time twelve o'clock midnight.

"Dad, you mean to tell me you're not going to set a time? Oh, no. That's not what happened when I went to the prom. You scared the dead out of my date."

"Carlene, this is a new generation. Dad knows that I'm responsible and I know when my curfew is."

"Junior, I don't care... it's not fair. Your curfew is midnight! I'll be sitting up waiting for you!"

Junior pulled Carlene into the kitchen. "Cool it girl... you trying to mess me up. How much money do you want to shut your mouth?"

"I don't want nothing... but since you insist give me twenty bucks!"

"Carlene, twenty bucks!? You know I don't have that now... come on. I tell you what, I give it to you when I come back from the prom."

"Don't forget or I'll... mess... you... up!"

"Shush… be quiet. You will get your money!"

"What are you and Junior whispering about?" Virginia asked.

"Nothing, Mom!" I'm just fixing his tie.

Junior and Randolph left to pick up the girls, saying that they will come back by the house for Carlos to take some more pictures. Carlos told the boys not to get in any trouble and wished them a good time. Carlene told Virginia that it's not fair the way dad treated Junior on his prom night. Virginia informed Carlene that she agreed with her, but her father has very good intention and that's to protect his little girl from making the biggest mistake of unwanted sexual encounter and pregnancy. "You should know by now that it is the greatest fear of any parent of girls. Boys can also encounter the same impact, but the child of a boy doesn't become the full responsibility much as it will affect the girl. Now, that's how your father feels about his children's sexual encounters. One day, when you have a family of your own, you will confront the same issue and then you will understand your father's motives. Fathers who have a daughter want the best for their child. That's why I will not interfere because I know and understand his methods on handling this issue. Believe it and you should be thankful that you have parents who have your best interest at heart."

Junior and Randolph (who was white) arrived at the Slaughter's home with their dates along with Junior's best friend, Jerry (who was also white). Virginia, Carlos, and Carlene were delighted to see the teens dressed in their prom attire. Carlos took pictures of the teens, and they all departed to attend their prom.

Later that night, Junior called prior to midnight to tell Carlos that his date and peers wanted to go to Denny's Restaurant. Carlos approved and told Junior to be careful driving home.

Junior arrived home at two o'clock in the morning. Carlene was up downstairs in the family room. She teased Junior about the time, indicating that she was going to tell dad what time Junior came in. Junior told her that won't be necessary because he called dad and he gave his permission to take Tasha to Denny's. Carlene revealed that she knew he called and wanted to tease him.

The next morning, Junior shared his night out with his date and thanked his parents for letting him use the car. Carlene told her brother to pay up. Junior placed the money in Carlene's hands and Carlene returned the money. Carlene said that she just wanted to see if he would pay up and was glad her brother had a good time. Junior told his parents that Jerry mentioned last night that he got a job in repair and roofing house for the summer and offered him to contact his uncle to apply for a vacancy position that was still open. Carlos was surprised and realized Junior took responsibilities of his life. Virginia and Carlos told Junior to go apply.

"Mom and Dad, I'm serious about getting the money to buy me a used car."

"Son, once you have saved some money, your mother and I will keep our word to assist you to buy a car, but not until you can save the money. I had to work and save money to purchase my first car and I'm glad that my parents allowed me to purchase my own car because it taught me to be a responsible young man and I took care of my vehicle, because I worked hard to purchase a new car. I didn't participate in sports at the high school age. I started working at the age of fifteen and been working to this date. If you don't believe me, just ask your mother."

"Dad, I already know about your childhood from Grandma, and your first car was a Volkswagen."

"Well... I just want you to know that it's very important to work and earn your wants, needs, and desires."

Carlene returned to college leaving Carlos and Junior to deal with Virginia's loss. Carlos told Virginia that if she wants to discuss her grief, he's available to listen and give Virginia space to cope with the vision of change in her life.

CHAPTER SEVEN

CHANGE ADJUSTMENT

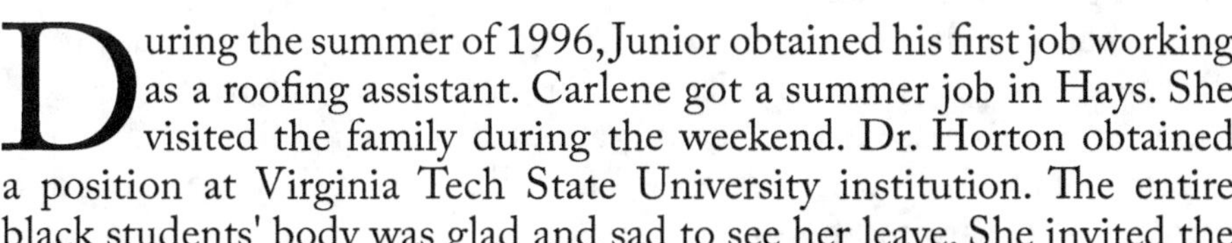

During the summer of 1996, Junior obtained his first job working as a roofing assistant. Carlene got a summer job in Hays. She visited the family during the weekend. Dr. Horton obtained a position at Virginia Tech State University institution. The entire black students' body was glad and sad to see her leave. She invited the students to visit her in Virginia where she was settled.

Junior saved enough money to purchase his vehicle, but Virginia was not in a hurry to get Junior his car, so assisting Junior to open a savings account to put his money until they purchase his car. Of course, Junior was very upset, but knew that his parents had his best interest at heart. Virginia feared the peer pressure her son would encounter and decided to wait until Junior graduated from high school. Virginia's vision of today's generation was very challenging and destructive than the '70s or earlier generation. Purchasing her son a car could expose him to challenging issues that he could not handle such as drugs, gang, sex, etc. She provided Junior with study materials to prep for college entry. She told Junior how important it was for him to be focused on what direction he wanted to take once he graduated. Virginia enlightened her son on what his options were— college, civilian employee (limited due to lack of skills and experience), or military enlistment. Junior indicated that he wanted to go to college, but also may be interested in joining the military. Junior revealed his direction, and Virginia ensured that her son's options explored. Virginia contacted the resources, and assisted Junior in implementing his options. Junior met the average score level entry for community colleges. Virginia informed Carlos to contact the recruiter in the area for Junior to explore the offers of the military. Carlos felt that his son was not interested in higher education. He didn't see the enthusiasm Carlene had at Junior's age. Carlos saw Junior's uncertainty and his desires to hang with peers and his lack of responsibility initiative of setting further goals. Virginia disagreed, saying that, of course, Junior's behavior was different from Carlene, but insisted that, as parents, they give Junior the opportunity to explore whatever his decision was and wish him success and, that's what she planned to do. Hearing his wife respond, Carlos contacted the recruiting office and made an appointment for Junior to be interviewed.

The 1996 school year began. Junior was now a senior in high school. Virginia enrolled at Central Texas for the fall semester. Carlos told the family that he was going to retire instead of going to Korea since he was eligible to. Virginia had mixed feelings about Carlos decision, but supported his decision. Carlos prepared himself for retirement by prepping for civilian employment.

Cheryl called Virginia, informing Virginia of her husband's decision to retire due to military changing in mission tasks. Both of the women discussed their feeling about not having the opportunity to relocate at government expense, but realized that they are aging and wanted to live around family.

Junior's grades met the requirement to participate in playing basketball. Virginia told Junior the minute his grades drop, he should stop playing sports. Junior was becoming interested in girls. Virginia and Carlos attended Junior's games supporting their son. Carlos notices a change in his son's behavior fearing that he may have an interest in alcohol or drugs. Looking back at his childhood, Carlos recall how his peers influenced his decision in alcohol and drugs and feared that his sons may be experiencing the same peer pressure, therefore he became focus in his son peers and environment. Virginia was still coping with the loss of her father and now her mother's illness hasn't improved, therefore, she was blind to her son's behaviors and moods. Junior's and Carlos's relationship as father and son became very challenging due to Carlos's determination not to allow his son to destroy himself.

The year of 1997 arrived, a year that will change the Slaughter's household forever. This was the year that both their children will be graduating, Carlene from college and Junior from high school. Carlene's grades met the requirement to enter the master's program. Carlene visited her parents one weekend and told them of her goals to further her education. She mentioned that she contacted Dr. Horton who invited her to Virginia to check out Virginia Tech's master's program and she wanted her mother to join her on this trip. Carlos was enthused that Carlene had made the decision to continue her education and invited Virginia. He knew that his wife needed another focus to get her mind off her mother's illness, which she could not control. Carlene told Virginia that some of her college friends, who were her mother's age, will be going to Virginia to visit Dr. Horton.

In the month of March, the girls flew to Roanoke, Virginia, airport. Dr. Horton greeted and picked Carlene and her mother up at the airport. She told them that Arlene and Vicki arrived yesterday and was waiting at the house. She ensured the girls that they will enjoy their trip. The ladies arrived at Dr. Horton's beautiful home in the Valley of Blacksburg, Virginia. Virginia called Carlos and Junior to inform them of their safe and pleasant trip.

Photo by EpicV27 (Own work) [GFDL (http://www.gnu.org/copyleft/fdl.html) or CC BY-SA 4.0-3.0-2.5-2.0-1.0 (https://creativecommons.org/licenses/by-sa/4.0-3.0-2.5-2.0-1.0)], via Wikimedia Commons

Meanwhile, Carlos and Junior were at home missing the girls. Virginia and Carlene unpacked and joined the ladies in the family room. The ladies discussed their flight and agenda of enjoyment Dr. Horton planned for the girls. The next day, the ladies toured Virginia Tech campus. The ladies were very impressed of the university and what it offered. They attended an evening dinner event the college had for student's visiting the campus. The ladies enjoyed an evening of dancing and laughter. Dr. Horton guest were the highlight of the evening. The staff were pleased that her radiant women guest decided to attend the event. The rest of the week the women visited the shopping area and finish their tour of Virginia Tech State University. The ladies told Dr. Horton how attractive the offer of attending Virginia Tech was as a selection university to achieve their goals in receiving their masters. Virginia indicated her support if Carlene chose to attend Virginia Tech, and Dr. Horton ensured her support to care for Carlene.

The date arrived for the ladies to depart the area. Dr. Horton took the ladies to the airport. They boarded their plane and returned to their residence. Carlos and Junior were glad the girls returned. The girls shared their adventure. Carlos asked Carlene's decision. Carlene said that she wanted to check out Hays's master's degree program before she made a final decision.

Virginia received a call from Personnel Service Battalion announcing she was selected to join their department as a Personnel Management Assistant. Virginia was excited and told her colleagues and supervisor of her new employment. Virginia's supervisor was sad but happy that Virginia's goals were met in her career. That evening, Virginia contacted Carlos and friends about her new job.

Two months later, Virginia received a call from Tricia, saying that her mother's condition had not improved and was transferred to a hospital in Atlanta for further testing. Tricia said that she will keep her updated with her mother's condition and gave Virginia her mother's room number. Virginia told Tricia that she was going to make arrangements to visit her mother that summer. Virginia called her mother and she indicated that she was doing fine, and the doctor had a minor testing procedure he wanted to explore. Virginia called her aunt Marilyn to discuss her mother's condition. Aunt Marilyn told Virginia that they were just exploring their options to pinpoint her mother's illness due to the long-term care and treatment not helping her recovery. Aunt Marilyn said that she will contact Virginia once they have the results of her mother's test.

The month arrived for the Slaughters' big day, Junior's prom and graduation for Carlene and Junior. Virginia and Carlos had a lot of preparations for their children. Virginia's plate was full, coping with two graduations thanking God that the events were two weeks apart. It was prom night and Junior's date was a white girl. He told his parents one week prior to the event because he didn't know how they would react. Virginia and Slaughter didn't respond any different than if his date was a black girl. Junior was pleading to see the positive reaction from his parents. Virginia told Junior that it's not the color, race, or appearance of an individual; it's the character and moral value that's important. As long as her children are happy with their relationships, Virginia can accept and welcome the individual into the family. Virginia selected the floral for Junior's date and Carlos assisted Junior in selecting his tuxedo attire. Junior gets dress for prom and goes to get his date and bring her to his home. Junior introduces his date, Jennifer, to his parents. Junior retrieved the floral from the dining room table. Carlos and Virginia watched as Junior placed the floral on his date's wrist. Carlos took pictures of the couple, and they wished their son a successful night. Carlos reminded Junior about the rules. Just as Carlene was getting ready to leave, she called Junior asking questions about his tuxedo and his date. Junior addressed her questions and handed the phone to Virginia. Carlene informed Virginia that she had made their hotel reservation for her graduation and sorry she could not be there to see her little brother attend his last prom. Virginia handed the phone to Carlos who said hello and a quick good-bye so he can take pictures. Junior told his parents that they will eat breakfast at Denny's after the prom. After the prom, Junior called his parents to confirm eating at Denny's with his date and friends.

A week later, the Slaughter family went to Hays for the big event—Carlene's receiving her bachelors of arts. Two days prior to Carlene's graduation, Grandma Slaughter's flight arrived at the Kansas Airport in Missouri. Carlos and Virginia were there to greet Mrs. Slaughter. The day before Carlene's commencement ceremony, the family arrived in Hays. This was an exciting moment. This is the first grandchild to graduate from college. Mrs. Slaughter is a proud grandmother and very glad that God had bless her to be a part of this event. The family attended the graduation ceremony sitting among the crowd, applauding Carlene as she walked across the stage to receive her diploma. This is a day the Slaughter family will never forget. This day exemplifies their superior performance of parental guidance. One week later, the Slaughter gathered to attend Junior's graduation ceremony. Carlos is proud of his children and his wife of their achievement as individuals and support they bestowed toward his career. They faced many challenges to achieve these goals, but, in the end, the reward was worth the battle. Mrs. Slaughter returned to Georgia one week after her grandchildren's event experiencing an adventure that will last forever.

One week after graduation, Carlos and Junior went to pick out Junior's car. Junior picked out a used Honda Civic. They both returned home with his car. Virginia came out of the house and looked at the car. Junior asked his mom's opinion, showing his her his car. Junior thanked his parents for helping him pay for his car. Virginia told Junior that he better take care of his car because the next car will be Junior's responsibility to pay in full without additional financial assistant from his parents. Junior was very excited and took his car for a spin. Weeks later, Carlos and Virginia were asking Junior about his career future. Junior had no clue to what he wanted to do. One minute, he said he's going to join the military and the next day he is going to attend college, but one thing was sure, Junior enjoyed hanging out with his peers, and Carlos and Virginia knew that their son was not focusing on his goals. They both feared that their son would get caught in drugs and alcohol by hanging out with friends and decided something needed to be done before it got out of control.

Summer arrived and Junior was all set for seeking employment, but Carlos had other things in mind for him. Carlos realized that his son needed a glimpse at what the world has to offer and the only way Carlos can ensure his son's future was to give him a taste of the ghetto. Junior, like other teens of the era, dressed with sagging pants. Carlos and Virginia informed Junior that his attire must change if he wanted to seek employment and be successful. Today's youth are hung up on today's fashion, not realizing in order to be successful, an individual's image bestows lasting impressions to their employer. Carlos and Virginia had often told Junior that maturity and appearance was one tool young adults must acquire in order to be successful in the professional business career. Knowing this, Carlos decided to send his son to Macon to expose him to the lifestyle and environment of the unsuccessful. Carlos presented Virginia with this idea and she agreed. Junior was furious when his parents told him that he will not be hanging out or seeking employment before attending college. Carlos called his mother and informed her that Junior will be spending a few weeks in Macon prior to college.

Carlos and Junior flew to Georgia. When they arrived in Macon, Carlos escorted his son to the ghetto and his peers who were not successful. He exposed his son to the impact of drugs and alcohol among relatives and friends. He wanted his son to know the worst that can happen to his life. He told him, "This is his life—your choice and your future." Leaving Junior with this thoughts, Carlos returned to Kansas giving him plenty to think about when he returns to Kansas. Junior hung out with cousin Kirk and other relatives and friends getting a glimpse of their lifestyle in a big city living in the ghetto or low-income environment. Carlos and Virginia periodically call home to check on Junior. Junior had a lot to discuss in reference to poverty and unsuccessful individuals and was glad his parents gave him the opportunity to explore the lifestyle of an unsuccessful individual.

Junior returned on two months later with a clear Vision of Change about his future. He told his parents that he decided that he wanted to attend Johnson County Community College in Kansas, City. Carlos and Virginia were proud that his son had finally realized what he must do to be successful. Being a parent of the present generation was very challenging. Parents were struggling to maintain parental guidance in the growth of their children due to drugs, gangs, sex, substance abuse, etc. In order to survive, parents must learn the method of raising their children. Disciplining children were constantly changing due to child abuse, but that does not mean every case is an abuse nor did it mean parents should not spank their children. If parents focused on raising their children in their early childhood, there is hope for the future of young adults. But children were raising themselves due the lack of guidance from their parents. Parents must focus on how to be successful parents as well as achieving their career goals in order to reach the "vision of change" their hearts desire.

CHAPTER EIGHT

THE LAST GLANCE

Carlene returned home three weeks before Junior went to college. Carlene and Junior spend a lot of time together.

The day has arrived for the Slaughter to go to Kansas City to look for an apartment for Junior and Jerry, who were attending Johnson County Community College. The young adults and parents arrived in Overland Park, Kansas, where the boys chose their apartment. The parents were anxious because they know their life is changing. Letting go of them and giving them the opportunity to fly away, wishing them great success. Junior and Jerry loved their apartment and discuss how their parents can help decorate. Junior and Jerry's parents discuss what they will provide to decorate the boys new home.

Weeks later, Carlene and Junior departed for their new adventure—attending college. Carlos and Virginia went with Junior to help him settle in his new home. The boys' parents bond together in assisting their financial needs. Once the boys were settled, their parents said their good-byes. Carlos and Virginia constantly call their children to ensure their safety. One week after Virginia arrived home from Overland, she received a call from Tricia saying that Mrs. Cottingham's illness had gotten worst and Virginia needs to come home. Virginia told Carlos and departed for Macon.

Virginia arrived in Macon finding her mother critically ill. The doctors insisted that Mrs. Cottingham needed twenty-four-hour monitoring. Virginia and her siblings decided the time had come to admit their mother to a nursing home. Mrs. Cottingham was released from the hospital. Virginia visited her mother and they discussed her health condition. Mrs. Cottingham ensured her daughter not to be concerned about her illness but requested Virginia to be available for her siblings and niece upon her death since she was the oldest. Virginia sadly agreed to be available for her siblings and niece, but implied that no one could ever replace a mother's love; still she will do her best. At Mrs. Cottingham's beside, Virginia and Tricia spoke of their mother's battle to hang on to life, but whispered to Mrs. Cottingham while wiping tears from her eyes, to let go the pain, saying that they were going to be alright.

Virginia and Tricia left the hospital and returned to Mrs. Cottingham's home. Virginia informed Tricia that it will take time for them to prepare for the death of their mother while they were not emotionally disturbed. Virginia and Tricia visited Jones Funeral home where they processed the funeral arrangement. The ladies agreed the best method of dealing with the death of a loved one, especially a mother, was to prepare before the death. The girls told their brothers and relatives what they planned to do. They informed their relatives that it's best to do it now because they will not be able to prepare at the time of their mother's death. Virginia arranged for her mother to be admitted to a nursing home and visited her mother for the *last glance of life*.

Virginia returned to Junction City to wait for the death or the miracle of life for her mother. Carlos and Virginia's lifestyle changed. Their children had flown away from their home to focus on their future, and the Slaughters had time to bond and grow in their relationship and career, building a strong everlasting foundation.

Months later in Hays, Carlene and Kevin were in a car accident. Carlene was seriously injured and rushed to the hospital. Mr. Horton called Carlene's parents to inform them. The Slaughters rushed to depart Junction City, driving to Hays. They arrived at the hospital and went to the emergency room. The receptionist told them of their daughter's conditions. Kevin was driving Carlene's car at the time of the accident and was being treated for minor injuries. He was in the emergency room lobby when Carlene parents arrived. Carlos and Virginia approached Kevin for questions about the incident. Minutes later, Mr. Horton came out into the lobby, sadly informing the Slaughters that the doctor was treating Carlene. She told the Slaughters that Carlene injured her leg because the car struck on the passenger's side, and the rescue team had to pry the door open to get Carlene out of the car. Carlene's car was totaled. Kevin told them that he was not at fault. The Slaughters were glad of the information, but their concern was how intense were Carlene's injuries. Kevin said that Carlene was in a lot of pain. Hearing the news, the Slaughters panicked, and Carlos insisted to see his daughter.

Moments later, the nurse came out from the emergency room, saying that they were transferring Carlene to room 319 located on the third floor. The doctor will be out to discuss Carlene's injuries and treatment. Thirty minutes later, Dr. Hudson came out and told the Slaughters that Carlene crushed her femur and required surgery, but due to her high blood pressure, they cannot perform surgery that night. The Slaughters thanked the doctor for the information, and they went upstairs to their daughter's room. Carlos stopped at the receptionist's desk to call Junior and tell him about Carlene. Then Carlos and Virginia entered their daughter's room in tears, seeing Carlene hooked up to those machines. Carlene was heavily sedated but aware of her parents' presence. Virginia noticed that Carlene was given morphine due to severe pain.

"Carlene, I heard that you and Kevin were drag racing on the highway. I have told you about racing. You got to rank among the pros to race."

"Dad... only you would say something like that."

Carlene smiled.

"Baby, mom is here and I'm not going to leave you here tonight. Matter of fact, I'm going to let the nurse know. Everything is going to be alright. You just rest and don't pay your father any attention you know he just want to humor you." She kissed Carlene on the forehand.

The nurse came into Carlene's room to check her vital signs. "How are we feeling?"

"I'm in a lot of pain," said Carlene.

"I know the medication should make you feel better. I'm going to give you a shot to help with the pain."

"Okay!"

"I will be staying overnight in my daughter's room. Do you have a bed cart for me to sleep on?" Virginia asked.

"No... but that chair in the corner lets out into a bed. I'll get you a blanket because these rooms are cold, if you want one."

"Oh, please... thank you!"

"It's getting late and I'm going to drive back to Junction City." Carlos kissed his girls and left.

The nurse brought a pillow and blanket for Virginia to stay overnight. Carlene's classmate and friend Tiffany entered the room. She asked Virginia about Carlene's condition and told her that she can stay in her place. Virginia told Tiffany that she will be staying in

Carlene's room and said that Carlos had gone back to Junction City and will return with Junior tomorrow. She thanked Tiffany.

During the night, in Carlene's room, Virginia noticed the IV was not flowing with fluid and Carlene was in pain. Virginia immediately paged the front desk for nurse assistance. The nurse came into the room and immediately changed the IV and checked Carlene's vital signs. Virginia asked the nurse about Carlene's conditions. The nurse told Virginia that everything was alright and thanked her for paging the front desk. Virginia noticed that Carlene still had high blood pressure and asked. The nurse said that she will inform the doctor and mentioned that Carlene also has a lot of swelling in her leg, which was not good, saying that she will report this in the morning.

The nurse left the room and Virginia knelt down alongside her bed to pray for Carlene. That morning, the nurse and doctor came into Carlene's room to conduct their examination. Dr. Hudson told Virginia that they cannot wait and must prep Carlene for surgery immediately. The doctor and nurse left Carlene's room. Virginia approached Carlene's bedside and kissed Carlene on the forehead. Virginia knew that Carlene's surgery would be risky due to Carlene's high blood pressure and told her to have faith in God. One hour later, Carlos and Junior entered Carlene's room. Tears began to flow from Junior eyes as he approached his sister bedside.

"Sis, everything is going to be alright... I'm here with mom and dad. So, you hang in there." Junior kissed Carlene's cheek.

The nurses entered the room to take Carlene to surgery. She told the Slaughters that the procedure should take two hours. Virginia told the nurse that they will be waiting in the patient lounge. The Slaughters stood in the corner of the room and waited until the nurse rolled Carlene out! Yelling, "Hang in there, Carlene! We love you!"

Carlene smiled and whispered "okay" as she was taken to be prepped for surgery.

Just as the Slaughters were leaving Carlene's room, Tiffany and Dr. Horton came to check on the status. Virginia informed them that she had been taken to surgery. Tiffany asked if they have seen Kevin.

"No, we have not seen Kevin nor did he come up to the room last night. Where is Kevin?"

"I don't know. But I do know that he and Carlene broke up. That's why I'm surprised he was driving her car."

"Broke up? Carlene never told us that they were not seeing each other!"

"Oh... forgive me. I thought you all knew."

"Don't be sorry. I'm glad you told us. Now that explains his behavior."

"Well, bump the boy's behavior. I'll speak with him later. I have a few words to say to that young man. He could at least show some respect where my daughter is concerned."

"I agree. But not surprised. I thought you all knew that they had broken off their relationship. That was the best thing Carlene could have done. She was going to move back into the dorm this weekend."

Carlos was furious. The Slaughters, Dr. Horton, and Tiffany went down into the cafeteria to get something to eat. Virginia didn't want to stand in line and asked Carlos to just get her a glass of orange juice and seated herself at a table while the other got in line and ordered their breakfast.

While eating their breakfast, Carlos asked Tiffany further about Carlene and Kevin. After they finished eating, Carlos asked Tiffany to take him to Kevin's place to get his daughters things. Carlos and Junior left while Virginia and Dr. Horton stayed in the patients lounge to wait on the status of Carlene.

Carlos and Junior arrived at Kevin's apartment. Kevin was not at home. Tiffany had Carlene's keys and got out of her car to open the door. Carlos and Junior went into the apartment with Tiffany and gathered up Carlene's belongings. The guys loaded Carlos's truck with Carlene's things, thanked Tiffany, and left.

They returned to the hospital lounge, hoping to hear good news. Virginia told them that they have not heard any news yet. Minutes later, the nurse came into the lounge and told the Slaughters that Carlene's femur was crushed; therefore, the surgery will be longer than two hours. She said that Carlene's vital signs were okay. Hearing the news, Virginia silently left the lounge and headed to the chapel. In a daze, she entered the room, pouring down in tears, kneeling at the altar, praying for her daughter. Carlos noticed Virginia leaving and assumed that Virginia went to the ladies' restroom.

Dr. Horton and Tiffany left telling Carlos and Junior they will be back in a couple of hours. Minutes later, Virginia returned to the lounge. Carlos asked Virginia's whereabouts, saying that he was going to ask the nurse to check the ladies' restroom because she was gone for a long time. Virginia, in tears, said that she went to the chapel to say a pray for Carlene, praying that this will not be the *last glance* of her daughter's face.

"Mom... Carlene had been in surgery for least four hours. Nothing better happen to my sister. Kevin better not come here."

"Junior... this is not the time or place to be concerned about that boy. We need to focus on saying a pray that Carlene will survive this surgery."

"Mom... I did pray... and I'm still praying, but I better not see Kevin right now."

Six hours passed, the nurse reported to the lounge to give the Slaughters the news that Carlene survived the surgery and was in the Intensive Care Unit. She told the family once they got Carlene settled, she will allow them to see her. The nurse returned to the ICU. Minutes later, the nurse went to the patients lounge to retrieve the family and escort them to the room. The Slaughters were in tears seeing Carlene on several machines. Junior asked the nurse when she will wake up. The nurse said that she is heavily sedated. The Slaughters gathered around her bedside whispering words of faith and love. Carlene slowly opened her eyes.

"Mom, Dad, Junior... I hear you and love you all too!"

The Slaughters looked at Carlene with a smile, saying, "We love you too." The doctor came into the room told the family about the surgery and the damage of the femur and how they repaired the damages. He said that Carlene will be on crutches but will not need a cast. It will take a while before she will be back to her activities, assuring a successful recovery.

The Slaughters left the hospital to get something to eat and register at the Comfort Inn Hotel. Meanwhile at the hospital, Dr. Horton and Tiffany went to see Carlene. Minutes after Dr. Horton and Tiffany left, Kevin went to visit. Later that evening, the Slaughters returned and the nurse mentioned that Kevin just left. Virginia told Carlos and Junior to stop getting upset over Kevin. "God will take care of him; besides, we have not spoken to Carlene, therefore, we shouldn't pass judgment until we have spoken to her, and this is not the time to discuss this issue."

Later that evening, the Slaughters visited Carlene to tell her that Virginia will be staying and that Carlos and Junior will be returning to Junction City. Dr. Horton and Tiffany assisted Virginia during her stay. The doctor released Carlene on Friday of that week.

Virginia and Carlene returned to Junction City where Carlene continues her recovery from the accident. Once Carlene was settled at home, Virginia and Carlos addressed the accident and Carlene's and Kevin's relationship. Carlene told her parents that Kevin was helping her move her things back into the dorm because they had broken off their relationship. Carlene said that Kevin had issues that she could not accept. Evidently, according to Carlene, Kevin didn't know what his future goals were and he used drugs. Carlene said that he had been using drugs and the rumor got out among the students and Carlene discovered the evidence in his apartment. Carlene said they were going to his apartment when they were hit by a trucker trailer.

Weeks later, Virginia had a strange dream. Virginia's dream revealed her deceased father sitting on the stairs in the hall doorway. Mr. Cottingham's spirit directed Virginia to sit next to him. In the dream, he was comforting Virginia and telling her that everything will be alright. The next day, Virginia awakened and shared her dream with Carlene. She said that Mr. Cottingham was dressed in black overalls and carried a backpack. Virginia was very disturbed about the dream. Carlene told her mother it's just a dream, besides grandfather probably just want to see you and did through your dream. Later that evening, Virginia received a call from Tricia saying that Mrs. Cottingham had passed away. Virginia bursted into tears asking questions surrounding her mother's death. Virginia immediately hung up the phone and told her family. Carlos embraced his wife allowing her to cry on his shoulder. Virginia said that she must leave immediately so she can prepare for the funeral. Carlene saw the emotional imbalance her mother presented and decided that she was going to fly with her mother. Virginia mentioned to Carlene that she was in no condition to fly because she was still recovering. But Carlene insisted that she will be alright, so Virginia scheduled a flight for two. Carlos called Junior to inform him of his grandmother's death. Carlos and Junior will drive to Georgia because Junior must have time to prepare for his departure from college. Junior told his roommate and teachers of his family's crisis.

Virginia packed her clothes, continuing to cry over the loss of her mother. There were no words anyone could say to relieve the pain. Carlene and Carlos remained silent and only spoke if Virginia addressed an issue or needed assistance. Carlos drove the girls to the Kansas Airport. That was the longest and saddest ride Carlos and Carlene had ever ridden with Virginia. Virginia continued to wipe the tears of sorrow from her face as she stared at the highway from the passenger front seat in their car.

They arrived at the airport and Carlos kissed his wife good-bye. He kissed Carlene and told her to take care of her mother and he and Junior will be down later. Virginia and Carlene arrived at the Atlanta Airport. Tricia and Bro greeted the girls. Bro was surprised to see Carlene. Carlene told them that she was not going to let her mother travel alone, especially under these circumstances. The Stewardess waved down a wheelchair for Carlene and they went to the Baggage Claim to retrieve their luggage.

During the drive to Macon from the airport, Tricia told Virginia of the last glance of her mother before her death.

"I visited mom at the nursing home and was braiding her hair and her head was as light as a feather," Tricia said. "She insisted that I call you so she could speak to you, but I told her that you were alright and I will tell you that she asked about you. I had no idea that she was dying and her last request was to speak to you. I'm really hurting because I should have called you, but I didn't know that she was dying."

"Tricia, why are you beating yourself over the last glance of mother's life. There was no way you could have known; besides, I had this strange dream about dad, and in the dream, I was very upset, and he was comforting me, saying everything is going to be alright. Now, I know what his message was all about. It was preparing me for mom's death."

The girls and Bro pulled into the driveway. Family and friends were gathering on the porch. Jones Funeral home had brought their equipment and purchased Kentucky Fried Chicken for the family. Virginia and Tricia were very pleased with their services. Virginia called Carlos to inform him of their arrival. Jermaine's son was among the family. Tricia and Shawn introduced Virginia to Jermaine's son who looked just like actor Taye Diggs. Virginia couldn't believe her eyes and said, "Oh, my God! boy, you look just like your dad, Jermaine. Have you heard from your father?"

"Yes, he writes me sometimes," said Jermaine Jr.

Carlene and Shawn were staring at Jermaine. Virginia stepped over to the girls who were sitting in the chairs on the porch across from him. Virginia waved her hands in front of Carlene and Shawn.

"Hello, what's the matter, Carlene?"

"Mom, he looks just like Taye Diggs."

"I told you, Carlene. You react just like I did when I first saw Jermaine."

"I don't mean to stare, but you sure do look good. Too bad you are my cousin."

"Yep, he's your cousin and don't you girls forget."

"Auntie, we are not going to forget," Shawn said. "Matter of fact, Jermaine Jr. can hang out with us anytime.

"Don't y'all let these crutches fool you. I still can move around. It may take me awhile to get to where I'm going, but I can move." Carlene smiled.

"It saddens me when I heard about your dad going to prison. Now, I hope you don't follow your father and get into trouble. What are your goals?"

"I want to go to college and major in business. My dream is to have my own business someday."

"That's good... and you can seek your goal by staying focused. Don't allow your peers steer you away from your goals. Carlene can give you tips and feedback about college life. Isn't that right, Carlene?" Virginia waved her hand again in Carlene's face.

"Oh... yeah, Mom. I'm sorry but I just can't get over him looking like Taye Diggs."

Just moments later, Rose and Ellie drove up in the driveway to see their beloved friend Virginia. Rose and Ellie walked up to Virginia embracing her.

"Virginia, I'm sorry that Mrs. Cottingham died. I told mama when I read the article in the paper," Rose said.

"Yep, I heard about the news from your cousin Debra," said Ellie. "I saw her in the store and she mentioned it to me. How are you doing?"

"Well, I just got here today and I'm trying to be strong and hang in there, girls, but it's very hard for me. Mama had been sick for a while and this was expected but still it's very hard to accept... that my mama is gone."

"Girl, I know it's hard," said Rose. "Is there anything that I can do?"

"Yes, Virginia, is there anything we can do?" asked Ellie.

"Well, no. I'm just glad to see you all and just keep me in your prayers because I'm definitely going to need all the prayer I can get to get through this loss."

"You don't have to ask that because you definitely will be among my prayers," said Rose.

"The same goes for me," said Ellie.

"Well, well, well." Rose said. "Look who else is driving up the driveway. It's the Popes. Mr. and Mrs. Pope."

Pat and Greg walked up on the porch and embraced Virginia. "Hi, Rose and Ellie. Long time since I've seen you all. How are you all doing?"

Rose said, "Girl, I've been doing fine and you?"

Pat answered, "I'm doing fine."

"What about you Greg?"

"I'm doing fine. I'm not likely to have known who you were, Girl! It's been a long time."

"Yes, it had been! It's sad that we all got to see each other under these conditions."

"Yep, I agree. "What's up, Pat?" Greg asked.

"What do you mean, what's up? Aren't you all still married?"

"No, Girl," Pat said. "We been divorced for years!"

"See? That goes to show that we haven't seen each other for a long time. I thought you all were still married. I thought I was the only one out of the bunch that was divorced."

"No, the only couples who are still together are Virginia and Carlos. Everybody around here is divorced, on drugs, alcoholic, or dead."

"Now, you are right about that. There are a lot of our classmates who are alcoholics or on drugs."

"What?" said Virginia. "Are you serious?"

"Tell her, Pat. A lot of the people who went to school are either dead or on that stuff!" said Rose.

"Yep, she's right. I call Virginia and try to keep her up-to-date on y'all classmates. You know I graduated a year before y'all did."

"That's right you did!" Rose said.

"Where my partner, Carlos?" Greg asked.

"Carlene and I flew down. Carlos and Junior are driving down tomorrow."

"Oh. Now is that's your daughter sitting over there?" Greg asked.

"Yep, that's Carlene!"

"Girl, she sure has grown, looking just like you, Virginia…. What happen to your leg?"

"I was in a car accident," Carlene said.

"Oh, I'm sorry to hear that. I guess I'm going to have to catch up with Carlos when he gets here."

Virginia and her friends continued to mingle among the family and friends catching up on the pass. Virginia and Tricia had their work cut out for them preparing for the eulogy of their mother. The girls were glad that they planned the arrangements earlier therefore they only have to make a few arrangements to finalize the eulogy. Mrs. Cottingham's sister, of course, wanted to address their input in reference to the eulogy.

Mr. Jones, the director of the funeral home, called Virginia to welcome her and said he has never received or seen this many people to visit their funeral home. Mrs. Cottingham was a well-known individual and he was glad to provide services for the family during their moments of grief.

"Thank, you Mr. Jones, for your assistance and excellent services."

Virginia received a call from Teddy's mother, Ms. Anita, expressing her condolence to the family. Ms. Anita said that she had no idea that Mrs. Cottingham was ill and showed her assistance to the family. Virginia thanked Teddy's mother for the call and lovely flowers.

Tricia was listening to the call. "That was nice of Ms. Anita to call."

"Ms. Anita and mom go way back. Matter of fact, they went to the same high school."

"Oh... I didn't know that."

"Yep, mom mentioned that to me when Teddy and I started dating. That's why mom was so fond of Teddy because she knew his family."

Virginia lay across the bed after Ms. Anita called reminiscing over the last year of her mother's life with Tricia. The girls laughed and cried as they recalled the days and the last glance of Mrs. Cottingham's life. Later that evening, the girls went to the funeral home to take Mrs. Cottingham's clothes. Mr. Jones invited the girls to go in their preparation room to see the remains of their mother. Virginia, in tears, slowly walked through the door with Tricia by her side. They viewed their mother's remains in tears, kissing her on the forehead. Mr. Jones gave the ladies a tour of the preparation room, revealing the embalming procedures of a body. He shared their procedures to protect the human body from decay. This was an experience the girls thought they would never explore, extending thanks to Mr. Jones. He said that they were very special individuals, and their family was very well-known and respected among the community.

"Our services are to provide the best quality services," Mr. Jones said. "We will not rush the family during the moment of grief. You girls can feel free to come and view the body at any time prior or after the dressing of your mother. I understand the need for family to visit and grant them the opportunity of the last glance as many times you feel the need to visit before the eulogy."

The girls left the funeral home with lasting quality impressions of Jones Funeral Home Services. The days were passing quickly to the moment the Cottinghams will say their goodbye to the fallen heroine, mother and soldier of the United States Air Force. Carlos and Junior arrived the day before the funeral. Carlos saw the stress and weakness in his wife eyes. He encouraged her to be strong providing her his shoulder to lean on. Mrs. Cottingham's sisters provided the escort services for the funeral travel session by the police department and extra limousines for Mrs. Cottingham's siblings. They wanted their sister's homecoming to be the best among the best as a soldier she served to fight for freedom for all mankind.

The day arrived and everyone gathered at the Cottingham home. This was one of the saddest days of Virginia's life. Virginia stood strong, setting an example for her siblings to follow. The families entered their vehicle and the escort directed the travel to the church. The family arrived and was greeted by family and friends. They had never seen these many people attending a funeral in their life nor did they know the popularity of their mother. Eulogy begins and the presiding pastor of the Eulogy was Mrs. Cottingham's Brother-in-law Dr. Hall. He spoke the passionate words of courage, selfish and undying love of Mrs. Cottingham's compassion for her family and the respect she had earned among the community. A special song was presented to the congregation by Mrs. Cottingham's sister and remarks were addressed by family and friends.

The moment arrived for the family to view the body. Virginia began to cry and tremble as Tricia walks along by her side to view The Last Glance of their mother's remains. Tricia screamed with sadness, "Mama, please don't leave me," as Virginia shout "Mama I love you and I'm going to miss you, rest in peace until we meet again!" Carlos walks alongside the girls grabbing Virginia to keep her from passing out escorting her back to her seat. Bro escorts his sister Tricia back to her seat. The girls had an emotional breakdown in tears and words of passion of love and loss of their fallen heroine and mother.

The family calmed down and the congregation was escorted out the church. Virginia and Tricia continued to cry as they traveled to the grave site. The United States Air Force gathered at the grave site playing 'Taps' as they presented Virginia with the flag of her mother.

The family left the grave site and returned to the church for the serving of dinner. Virginia and Tricia didn't have much of an appetite. Carlos and his children constantly provided comfort to Virginia. Virginia returned to her mother's home and continued to reminisce among family and friend of the existence of her mother's life.

A week later, Carlos called his friend Joyner to arrange a visit since he was in the area. Carlos gathered his family and took them to see one of their military friends. They arrived in Phoenix, Alabama, to visit the Joyner's. Virginia had a glow of joy when she saw her friend Benita. The visit with friends was the medicine Virginia needed to bring a smile to her beautiful face once again. During their visit, they discovered the challenges of illness that had embarked upon this family and a miracle blessing they bestowed from God who delivered

Joyner from the lupus. Hearing their story of deliverance and change of life, the Joyner's family overwhelmed the Slaughters. Virginia realized that families can survive the challenges of military life. Virginia and Benita both remember the days when their husband's best friends were abusing alcohol and now they have survived the thirst and freedom of abundance of a destructive disease. The reunion was one they will never forget.

After the Slaughters' visit, they returned to Macon to spend time with family and to disburse Mrs. Cottingham's belongings and estate. One week later, the Slaughters returned to Junction City to adjust to loss of the fallen heroine and love one they will never forget.

While traveling on the highway to Junction City, Carlos got another idea to cheer up his wife. He decided to stop in St. Louis, Missouri, to visit Renee Wilder. Carlos call Wilder before leaving for Macon and mentioned that he may stop on his way back from Macon. Carlos mentioned that he was tired and exits the highway to Comfort Inn hotel. The family entered the hotel making reservation for overnight stay. Once they unload their luggage and relaxing in their room, Carlos call retired Sergeant Wilder, Renee's husband. Renee informed him that Wilder was not at home and gives Carlos their address and directions to her apartment. Carlos was surprised that she gave him an apartment number. He was sure that Wilder had bought him a home by now.

The Slaughters left the hotel and go to visit Renee. They were shocked to see the apartment address was located in a low-income housing area. Virginia asked Carlos was he sure he heard Renee correct. Carlos said that he was positive this is the location. The Slaughters enter the apartment complex and knock on Renee's door.

"What's up? I see y'all found it," Renee said. "I was waiting by the phone to see if you all were going to have problems finding this apartment because you can't see it from the highway."

"No, I didn't have any problems. Once I got on I-70, I just followed your directions and drove straight to it."

"James is not home. He is over to his mother's house. I called him and told him that you all were in town. James spends a lot of time over to his mother house."

"Every time we call, you always saying he's at his mother's. Renee, what's up with that?"

"Carlos, James has really changed. Ever since he retired and we moved back home, he's become this new person. He smokes more marijuana than I do and he has high blood pressure."

"Come on now, Renee, you got to be kidding me, I know James is not on that stuff."

"Oh, yes, he is. I couldn't believe it myself, but he got back here and started hanging around his brothers and it has just changed. I couldn't take it anymore, so I got this place for me and little James. I know little James is going to hate he missed y'all, especially when I tell him that Carlene and Junior were with y'all. I'm in the church on the Usher board."

"Renee, why don't you call him now and tell him that I'm here, I bet you he will come over."

"I'll call, but he may not be over to his mother."

"What you mean? He may not be over to his mother's house. Are you and James together?"

"Carlos, that what I'm trying to tell you. James and I are married in name only. Now he will come by here to check on little James and I every day but leave because he said he can't leave his mother."

"Renee, that doesn't make any sense."

"I'm sorry, honey, for cutting you off like that."

"That's alright, go ahead and finish what you were saying."

"Renee, I can't believe that James has changed. When I called him, he never mentioned that y'all are not together."

Renee calls James and told him that Slaughter is in town. James asked to speak to Slaughter on the phone. Renee gave Carlos the phone while slightly glancing at Renee's apartment.

"You still haven't repaired your shrunk. I remember Carlos saying that James mentioned y'all had a lot of damage in your shipment."

"No, girl, I haven't done anything. I'm trying to get me a house. James thinks that I'm going to wait on him, but I'm not."

Carlos hangs up the phone.

"What did James say?"

"Oh, he says that he will be over."

"Now, y'all can see for yourself. Now, he is going to play that role with y'all, but I know better."

"Renee, can I use your bathroom."

"Sure, just keep straight down that hall and turn left."

Virginia went to the bathroom and observed the apartment. It was in a mess and very crowded. Renee had cramped all her furniture into this small apartment. Virginia noticed that there are no male items were in Renee's bathroom. The only thing she saw was Renee's personal items. It was true that Renee and James were not together. To confirm, Virginia wondered down the hallway and looked in the closet and noticed none of James's clothes were in the closet and little James's room was dark and nasty.

Virginia immediately returned to the living room, and minutes later, a knock at the door and Renee directed Carlos to open the door.

"Carlos answer the door, it's probably James."

Carlos opened the door, but it was Renee's girlfriend Pat. Pat walked into the apartment.

"Renee, who is this scavenger you have in here?"

"Excuse me," Carlos said. "We thought you were James."

"Pat, these are my friends who are passing through. We all knew one another when we were stationed in Berlin."

Pat walked in with a bottle of wine. "Oh, I'm sorry. I thought you were somebody Renee had picked up."

The Slaughters all glance at one another when the lady said that.

"Don't y'all pay Pat any attention," said Renee."

"Where is James?" shouted Pat?"

"Carlos called him and he should be knocking at the door in a few minutes. His mother doesn't live that far from here."

"Can I offer you all a drink?"

"No, that is alright," Carlos said.

"Virginia, you don't won't a glass of wine?"

"No, I'll pass."

"What about you, Carlene and Junior? I know Carlos doesn't drink."

"No, we will pass."

"Y'all are all grown up. So, what y'all doing? Stand up and let me see how tall you all are! Boy, Junior is taller than me, and Carlene, what happened to your leg?"

"I was in a car accident, but I'm doing much better now. My mother and I flew out to Georgia and her family met us at the airport and I needed a wheel chair, but now I'm walking. I still have a little pain, but I'm getting better."

"Virginia, yell, Carlos mentioned that your mother died and you all were traveling back from the funeral when he called. So, you are doing alright? Are you sure you don't won't me to pour you a glass of wine?"

"I'm sure, Renee. You and Pat go ahead."

"Alright, now... a knock at the door, it's James."

"What's up, man?" James greeted. "Oh, I'm sorry, man. You got the entire family here. Well, what's going on, Slaughters?"

"Nothing much, man," Junior said.

"Boy, you sure have grown, and look at Carlene! Girl, you don't look like that little girl in Germany."

"Hi, Mr. James," said Carlene.

"Mr. James.... Now you can call me James."

"See what I say?" Renee said. "He is smelling himself!"

"Renee, don't start okay? Hi, Virginia... Girl, you don't have no kids anymore. It feels good. So what y'all doing with yourselves, Carlene and Junior?"

Carlene said, "We both are in college."

Walks and sit next to Carlos on the couch. "That's good. I wish little James would have gone to college, but he just made it out of high school."

"No, tell the true... little James is just like his dad," Virginia said.

"What's up, Carlos? Hey, man, let's go outside. Is that your vehicle? Man, that's a nice ride. Let's go outside and show me your ride. Junior come on out with me and your dad."

The men went outside to chat and the ladies stayed indoors. The Slaughters were very glad to see their friends, but sad to see their lifestyle. After their visit, they headed back to the hotel. Virginia went to lie on the bed and Carlene and Junior entered their parents' room before returning to theirs the night.

"Carlos, I just can't believe how bad James and Renee looked. Do you think they both are on drugs?"

"Well, you saw for yourself how skinny James looked.

"Dad, I never would have thought James would lose that much weight," Junior agreed. "Mr. James got to be on something as skinny as he was looking. Dad, I noticed how you didn't say much and you asked questions about the neighborhood when we went outside."

"Hey, I just wanted to know what's up in the neighborhood. These days, you have driven-by shooting and gangs hanging out. You didn't see those guys hanging on the corner."

"Yeah, I saw them, Carlene. Dad told James, man, let's go back inside."

"Yep. Because I didn't know what was going down and I wanted to get your mom and Carlene and get the hell out of there. It would have been different if I didn't have my family and was visiting, but I didn't have any idea that they were living in those conditions. Man, James had really changed. I should have known something was wrong when he never did come visit us when he got back home. Renee was looking bad, too, gained all that weight and look like she don't groom herself at all.

"Yep, she looking bad and it don't make sense for them to be living in those conditions when they both are employed. But, when you drank and on drugs you can't acquire the comfort quality lifestyle. I thank God that I've always had set goals for this family's future."

"Mom, I'm glad you are an individual with dignity and respect for yourself and family. That's why we are highly educated because of your guidance. I thank God for you and Dad every day, even though dad was stricter with me than with Junior."

"Your dad and I didn't want you to become a pregnant teen or drop out. We wanted our children to have the opportunity to be successful in society. Your father didn't do twenty years in the military for nothing and I made sure that his twenty years of service were worth the sacrifice not only for continuous freedom of our nation, but for the family. Now, you all see that in order for you to have the best quality of life you got to want it and earn it. You have many retired service members who didn't have goals prior to entering the military nor acquire the knowledge over their years of service to set goals for themselves and family." The Wilders are an example of a family without faith, hope, and desire for a better future."

"Mom, I was just kidding when I mentioned dad's morals for female. Now, I know why his behavior with me was different from his behavior with Junior."

The Slaughter family thanked God for their new "vision of change" living a life of comfort with dignity, respect, and new beginnings. Carlos thanked Virginia for her support and faith, saving him from becoming a man with a lost soul.

CHAPTER NINE

MOVING ON

arlene has decided to return back to college at Hays to get her master's degree. Virginia and Carlos were concerned that maybe Carlene should sit out a semester because she was still on crutches and healing from the accident. But Carlene assured her parents that she will be fine, besides she had moved on the first floor. The Slaughters took their daughter back to Hays. Carlene told her dad to take care of mom and she will be calling her mother. Virginia assures her daughter not to worry.

Carlos returned to work and the unit was preparing for their annual exercise NTC training. Carlos decides that it was time he gets out of the military and submits his retirement notice to his commander. The commander was surprised and tried to encourage Carlos to stay, but Carlos states that too much has happened in the family and it's time for him to get out of the army. The commander mentions that he is going to be missed and asked will he stay in to assist with the departure for NTC training. Carlos agreed to arrange for his retirement date to meet the commander's request.

Virginia's grief for her mother lead Virginia to pour herself deeply into work and finished getting her degree in Business Management. Carlos told his wife that he will be retiring. Virginia was shocked but pleased with her husband's decision. The couple had mixed feelings about moving on as retirees, but realized it was time. The kids had become adults and they were getting older, albeit wiser. Carlos did not want to be separated from his wife anymore, so he decided to retire. Carlos also decided to become active in Freemasonry and was elected as Worshipful Master prior to getting out of the army.

In 1998, the Slaughters became retirees and Virginia received her degree in Business Management. Virginia returned to the Eastern Stars with an officer position assisting Cynthia Banner who was the Worthy Matron.

Carlos's career changed leads him to seek employment in Civil Service. This new adjustment was very challenging for Carlos. As a soldier, Carlos worked alongside many civilian employees providing assistance and leadership to the organization mission. But times have changed and moving on means new beginnings as well as challenges. Many soldiers may think that the transition from active duty to civilian after years of employment with the military is easy, but it's not. As a soldier, your day never ends, and as a civilian, your duty hours are eight hours or overtime hours. To Carlos these things were very hard to accept, but in time, he learned to not think like a soldier but as a civilian, whose hours each day come to an end. There are times when Carlos wished he was active due to the flexibility of time and duty hours working smart not hard. Many retirees have difficulty in adjusting to the civilian lifestyle, but eventually they adjust and become leaders for the US government or economy working to achieve the goals of the organization.

Virginia's transition from active duty to retiree brought change of not having to deal with relocating and exploring the different cultural lifestyle development and seeking employment. The time came for Virginia to focus on her career. The death of Virginia's parents brought motivation to establish a legacy in life as a spouse, mother, career woman, author, and all her skillful development had to offer to our society.

Virginia's career skills lead her to conducting briefings for the military soldiers who received Permanent Change of Stations or Reassignment orders. The levy briefing provided the soldiers information about their gaining installation. Virginia's briefings included gaining installation arrival dates, deferment, assignment instructions, immunizations, length of tour, flight departure, additional training duty or TDYs prior to PCS and how to gain access of the post facilities (Youth Center, employment, housing, and schools, etc.). Virginia was very surprised to see the low attendance of spouses who actually attended these briefings. These briefings were held to assist the family to a smooth transition. Spouses who did not attend these briefings have difficulty in learning how to adjust to their new environment. They became very stressed and depressed due to lack of information and communication network. In order to eliminate stress, the family must gain the knowledge of their new environment in order to prepare for their "vision of change," which will embark on their lives. Today's military is focusing on ways to eliminate the lack of communication between soldiers and family in hope to enhance family unity and stress that continuously destroys soldiers and their family.

The military implements the Married Army Couple Program also known as Joint Domicile Assignment for husbands and wives who are members of the armed forces. This program is designed to assist married couples to be stationed at the same gaining installations or in a radius of at least fifty miles.

Virginia became a mentor for the soldiers and their families working in the Personnel Service Battalion. Virginia enjoyed giving assistance to the soldiers and their family ensuring that they have all the information they needed to prepare for their reassigned destination. This career move bestowed Virginia with the knowledge of understanding the stress soldiers and families encounter on and off duty. Many spouses have a hard time coping and dealing with long hours of their spouses basically because they have no ideas the procedures of a soldier duty hours. A soldier's duty hours consist of Physical Training exercise, formations, guard duty, and performing their on-the-job duties. It also includes ensuring that they be accountable not only for their families but their colleagues' safety and needs on and off duty. Working in an organization among soldiers, Virginia got the opportunity to explore the needs of mission and tasks achievement to improve and enhance to be the best among the best to meet the needs of the armed forces providing freedom for all mankind. This experience brought strength of courage, respect, and greater love for the armed forces, husband, and marriage.

Virginia received a call from Ruby Steven who was the coordinator for the Martin Luther King annual event held at the Municipal Building. Ms. Steven was an activist of Black African American and President of the NAACP of Junction City for many years. Ms. Steven is also a retired high school teacher of Junction City High School where she inspired many youth of the Black African American Heritage. She sponsored this event for many years giving awareness to celebrate this day as a day on not a day off work. She spread the legacy of Dr. Martin Luther King's mission of continuous freedom of all mankind with emphasis on Black African Americans. All the auxiliaries among the communities participated in this event to ensure its years of success. Virginia thanked Ms. Steven for extending the invitation for support and assured her that the organization will definitely be there again this year. She later called Cynthia to inform her about Ms. Steven calls and they discussed plans for this annual event. This is one of Junction City's annual events when all Americans come together to pay tribute to Dr. Martin Luther King, a man who believed in hope for all mankind with the greatest of vision of change.

Months later, the Slaughters received a called from Hamilton Literacy announcing the release of Virginia's novel. The family was very excited and proud of Virginia's success. The release of the novel brought a new change in Virginia's life. She became a celebrity. The soldiers were very proud of Virginia and the success she had accomplished especially since the novel was written about the armed forces and their family struggle among the military communities. Virginia's distinguished accomplishment gained salute from many soldiers who among her presents who were aware of her achievement.

The Personnel Service Battalion during this year also had a Chain of Command ceremony for the arrival of LTC Harold Williams. This ceremony was a historic event held at the headquarters' grounds with cannons, carriages, and horses. Virginia loved attending these historic Chain of Command ceremonies, hearing the sounds of the cannons and charging of soldiers dressed in their historic uniforms on their horses and incoming officer riding in the carriages.

The battalion was preparing for their annual Adjutant General's Ball held at Riley's ballroom. Virginia was presented with the offer to participate in toasting hail of chain of command ceremony. This was an honor and Virginia accepted the invitation. Carlos was always glad to be among the midst of his fellow serviceman. It was like being among family, which he spent many years participating in these annual events.

The week of the event, Virginia's supervisor, Mr. Moon, decided that he would attend this event. Being a retired master sergeant and a civilian employee, he was inspired by Virginia's leadership and relationship with soldiers to attend this annual event. He embraced Virginia with all the personnel knowledge and overwhelmed with her timely management skills. Virginia was pleased with his support for the battalion and event. This was going to be the last AG Ball due to the restructure of the units, so this year's event was to be very special and a memorable event. The committee decided that they wanted to add a skit to the event festivities. One of the characters that they included among the skit was Mr. Moon and his daily performance among the PSB. Virginia got the opportunity to observe the skit and couldn't wait for the debut performance.

The day before the ball Virginia visited Design Creation Beauty Salon to get a glamour style for the occasion. Of course, this meant hanging out among many women conversations. One of Pamela's comedians, Marcy, was there telling her jokes as usual expressing her adventure as an active duty spouse. She reminisced about her night hanging out in the club on ladies' night and playing the slot machine. She discussed what it takes to be a strong black woman and how she was not about to let anyone or anything take her man. Her theory of a strong black woman is one who keeps her grove on and does not let anyone play her down, not even her spouse. The things a woman does to entice her man are also the things a woman must continue to do to keep her man exploring all the sexual desires of a man needs, and oral sex is a plus in today's sex desires.

Another issue women have today is finance and marital deception. A military spouse must have a general idea about setting future goals for their family. For instance, a soldier received orders for deployment or field duty assignment, that's responsible for the finance, and the spouse. A responsible spouse will pay the bills, make a deposit in a saving account, attend college during the soldier's absence, or get a hobby and buy survival needs for the family. An irresponsible spouse will spend all the money, may not pay a bill and forget saving, party and barely buy items the family needs for survival, and definitely have marital affairs. Where does this leave the soldier's mental state once he returns home from his duty assignment? Well, for one thing, he is very angry and wanted to kill the spouse. He may have lost his entire savings, which he intended to use for his retirement and is now considering getting a divorce. The soldier felt that all the hard work he had done was for nothing due to lack of support from his spouse. A soldier needed a woman who can manage his finances in his absence. Remember the soldier has a twenty-four-hour duty career providing freedom for all mankind, therefore in order for his life voluntary dedication to our country not to be vain, he needs the support of his loving spouse and family.

Women today need to focus on planning and setting goals for a successful retirement and it can be done, but you must stay focused, make sacrifices, and use your resourceful facilities to face the challenges of the military community. If you have problems with your marriage don't be afraid to seek assistance. They can help you identify the problem before it gets out of control. The key is keeping your relationship alive and remember we all make mistakes, but that does not mean that it cannot be forgiven. Healing is the key to forgiveness and in time wounds do heal.

Marcy said, "Now I can get nasty with my words of wisdom, but I won't because I've been there and done it all, and I'm telling you that there is a rainbow at the end that will last forever. We received our retirement checks every month and guess what, it's always on time. Virginia, now, when are you going to release your next book? I got a lot of information free of charge for your next novel."

"Marcy, I'm going to remember that. Matter of fact, you just gave me plenty of information to include in my next novel. You're awesome girl."

Marcy had the audience full attention and applause. Pamela commented to her clients, "Don't y'all pay her any attention, she's crazy."

But Virginia felt that Marcy was real and full of humorous conversation that had a positive influence for the ladies within the salon.

The night of ball arrived. Virginia and Carlos are dressed and got ready for a relaxing evening among their serviceman. Carlos went downstairs in Junior's room and finds a pair of Junior's Jordan snickers. He asked Virginia if their son was home. Virginia said she doesn't know. Carlos placed the shoes in Junior's closet assuming that Junior left his sneakers. Carlos commented Virginia on her elegant appearance and Virginia returned the comment. The Slaughters entered the Riley's ballroom commenting among themselves about the elegant ice sculptures and decorations the soldiers coordinated. They arrived early for the social event in the lounge and joined Virginia's organizational event. Carlos felt different not being in uniform but had his honoree pendant on his formal dress attire to display his outstanding achievements during his years of service.

The Slaughters mingled among the guest, Carlos drank his coke and Virginia drank a glass of wine. Virginia received many positive comments from the mingling guest about her novel. The time had arrived for the guest to go to the ballroom for the festivities. The evening included a LTG Timothy Maude, DCSPER as a guest speaker, dinner, skit, and dancing. The Adjutant General Corps Soldier of the Year, PFC Jessica Hess, and the NCO of the Year were also honored. The skit performance was awesome.

The soldiers did an excellent performance of the daily activities throughout the PSB. The table of Carlos, Virginia, and 1st Lieutenants Rogers was full of laughter and applause. Soldiers screamed out Mr.

Moon's name as the actor performing, his character stated, "Where are my soldiers? They haven't reported for work today. All I have are my civilians here. Oh, I'm not tolerating this today. I'm going to the LTC office to find out what is going on. Man, I just can't believe this unit sometimes and they won't allow me to hire more civilians."

They also performed the Chief of Standard Installation, Division Personnel System (SIDPERS), Ms. Shipman's daily activities of computer communication system download Reassignments. They had several computer operators stations monitor by soldiers rushing to meet the deadline to retrieve the Reassignment CAP cycle. The soldiers were experiencing problems with the system and Ms. Shipman demanded the CAP cycle report on her desk by the COB today. After the guest speaker's lecture and skit, the Slaughters danced and continued to enjoy their evening.

CHAPTER TEN

BUNDLE OF JOY

Over the years, the Slaughters had many memorable moments of joy that will last them a life time. The era in 2000 brought joyful challenges that changed this family's generation—the birth of their first grandchild, Virginia's challenges as an author, the graduation of Carlos and Virginia from Central Texas, Carlene's graduation from Fort Hays State University, and the cruise Carlos took Virginia on.

One evening, Virginia was resting in the family room and she received a call from Leon asking to speak with Junior. Virginia told Leon that Junior is living in the Kansas City area attending Johnson County Community College. Leon said that while visiting Junior's apartment last week, Junior mentioned he will be home again this weekend.

"Leon, what do you mean he will be home again this weekend? We've not seen Junior in weeks."

"I'm sorry, Virginia. I probably shouldn't have mentioned that... I thought Junior was stopping by the house when he visited his girlfriend at Kansas State University."

"What girlfriend? Are you telling me that my son is dating?"

"Ms. Virginia... I said too much already. I thought you knew. Anyway, please have Junior call me, if he stops by."

"Leon, I will tell him you called."

Leon left Virginia very puzzled. Virginia had no idea that her son was visiting KSU campus on a weekly basis for his girlfriend. Virginia immediately went upstairs and told Carlos. Carlos called Junior on his cell phone to track his whereabouts. Junior does not answer and Carlos left a message.

"Well, dear, there is really nothing we can do. The boy is grown, but I would at least want to know when he's coming to this area."

"Virginia, remembered a while back when we attended the AG Ball and I ask you had Junior been home."

"Yeah, I remember that now."

"Well, the reason I ask you that was because there was a pair of new Jordon snickers in the middle of floor in his room. I assumed then that he must have accidentally left them but know that I'm thinking Junior had been home. Virginia and Carlos went to Junior's room and opened the closet.

"The sneakers are gone!"

"So, he had been coming home during the day when we are at work."

"I'm going to bless that boy out. He's has been coming home and not telling us or spending time with us."

"He must be in love!"

"What do you mean in love? And with whom?"

Later that evening, Junior came home with his girlfriend, Vanessa, a white girl with long blonde hair and blue eyes. Slaughter and Virginia were glad to meet Junior's girlfriend, extending greetings and welcoming her into their home. Virginia asked Junior how long he had been in the area.

"Mom, Leon told me that he busted me out. I was going to tell you and dad, but I guess I forgot."

"What do you mean you forgot? No, one would forget something of this important?

"I'm sorry," said Vanessa. "But a part of this is my fault. Junior wanted to stop by on several occasions, but I work and we didn't take the time to do it."

"Well, I guess we will excuse the both of you."

Virginia went upstairs and left Junior and Vanessa downstairs. Junior got the family album and showed Vanessa his childhood photos. Virginia returned to the family room observing Junior and Vanessa flipping through the family photos. Vanessa cannot believe how Junior looked in his early years and the photos of all the sports he participated in. Carlos joined in and they all commented about the memorable moments of the early years of the family. Vanessa sat among the family listening to their joyful moments.

The time arrived for the commencement of Virginia, Carlos, and Carlene. Carlos decided that he didn't want to participate in the commencement ceremony. Instead he wanted to be among the crowd taking photos of his wife Virginia receiving her Business Management degree. Carlene and Junior were excited for their mother of many talents to finally experience receiving a higher education degree. The family cheered among the crowd as Virginia approached the stage to receive her degree.

"Mom, how does it feel to be a graduate at your age?" Carlene asked.

"I'm finally glad that it's over, and it feels good."

"Now, Mom, you know what this means you must keep going. I don't know how you do it juggling family, career, and education, but you did it."

"Faith in God is the key to my success!"

"Mom, I will never measure up to your success: loving mother, wife, successful in all achievements career and hobbies. I'm very proud to be your daughter, a branch from a strong structure."

"That is very sweet, but now that's enough about me. Next week is the great day when we celebrate your success receiving your Master at the age of twenty-four? You did it without a break... that's success.

"Mom, I could have never done that without your encouragement. I'm blessed to have you and Dad as my parent's. Without you and Dad support and encouragement, I would have never taken this path in higher education. My success is your great mentoring achievement as parent of a military brat!"

"Yep, that is exactly what you are called." They all laughed.

Two weeks later, the Slaughter repeated the commencement celebration of Carlene receiving her master's.

Months later, Carlos arranged for a getaway cruise to the Bahamas. Virginia was surprised when Carlos presented his wife with the packages. Within two weeks, they would be flying to Orlando, Florida, to board the *Princess* cruise ship to the Bahamas. The *Princess* is one of the latest ships that sail to the Bahamas. This was a five-day-and-four-nights Vacation. Virginia called Carlene in Hays to tell her about the getaway. Apparently, Carlos had already told the kids that he was planning a trip to the Bahamas and swore the kids to keep his secret.

The day arrived for the Slaughters to depart for Orlando, Florida. Carlos and Virginia flew out from Kansas Airport landing in Orlando at noon. They arrived and picked up their rental car and drove to the Holiday Inn Hotel. They unpacked, relaxed, and headed for the Kennedy Space Center. They arrived at the center for the tour. Virginia and Carlos enjoyed the tour of the aircraft shuttle viewing the inside model capacity and equipment supplies. It was amazing to see the gear aboard the aircraft. After their tour, they purchased gifts for friends and family. That evening they had a romantic dinner at a Seafood restaurant. The next day they turn in their rental car and were driven to the ship for departure. They board the ship at Port Canaveral and presented their check-in information. The line was very long and a tornado alert was announced. Carlos and Virginia were frightened that their departure may be delayed, but the announcement indicate that they will depart on time. Once aboard the ship, the service began. Waitresses were available for assistance bringing tropical drinks and beverages. They check into their cabin and boy it was compact but nice. They had laundry service available on the ship. Once inside their cabin Carlos immediately jumped on the bed to test it out inviting Virginia to join him. They both lied across the bed.

"Well, it's not a king side bed, like ours at home, so you will be close with no room to run."

Virginia laughed. "Boy you are crazy."

"Yep, I got everything you will need—bottle of wine, and I'm going to have the servant bring our ice bucket, my coke, and I just want you to relax and let me have my way, Dear."

The Slaughters explored their cabin, unpacked, and later left for the tour of the ship and safety briefings. The ship was huge with spa, gym, shops for food, casino, and more. Their navigation cruise trip included shopping in Nassau and Bahamas. This full-day adventure was a one-of-a-kind experience. It began with a 30-minute historical harbor cruise to the Paradise Island Ferry Terminal. From there, your guide will escort you to a reserved location on the beach—chair and towel included—and provided a meal coupon for lunch at the Dive In snack bar. Received a self-guided map, which will entitle you to the tour Discover Atlantis, the extensive marine habitat aquarium attraction at your leisure. Themed to the Lost City of Atlantis, this attraction was home to over 150,000 fishes, representing 200 species. They were free to enjoy the casino, shopping, or a self-guided walk through the Waterscape. The Slaughters also had a full day on the beach relaxing in the ocean water. On board the ship, they had an elegant night out dinner with their captain. Dressed in their formal attire, tasting champagne, photo picture with their captain and dinner. The evening events were relaxing on the top deck with food and disco dancing. They had an elegant experience on the *Princess*, an adventure they will treasure for a lifetime.

The day had arrived for the them to go home. Once they returned, they shared their adventures with their friends and family, encouraging them to take a getaway among the ocean waters.

Carlene received a call from Kansas University for a position at the University in their Upward Bound Program. Carlene screamed for joy saying it's about time for someone to contact her for a job. The Slaughters were full with bundles of joy for their daughter beginning career and wishing her great success.

The day had arrived for marketing of Virginia's novel. Virginia was contacted to attend a four-day conference at Valley Forge Hotel located outside of Philadelphia, Pennsylvania. Virginia flew to Philadelphia to attend this event. When she arrived, the services at the airport were great. Virginia had a limousine shuttle service available for her travel. Virginia arrived at the elegant Valley Forge Hotel and checked into her elegant suite. She unpacked and went to the floor to pick up her four-day conference agenda. The four-day conference event included seminar with expert on writing and marketing books. Virginia attended several seminars and met other authors and sold her books. One of the seminars Virginia attended was John Kremer, best-selling author of *1001 Ways to Market Your Books*. She also met with manuscript editors who provided assistance in the release of her next novel. This was a very educational adventure that provided Virginia success with the media and marketing of her novels.

In Virginia's leisure time, she visited the King of Prussia Mall. "Whatever your taste, whatever your style, whatever you want or need, the King of Prussia Mall has what you're looking for. From shoes to belts, pants to shirts, books to music, formal to informal, and a multitude of other gifts and gadgets, the King of Prussia Mall will fulfill your shopping needs." This two-story, two-building complex was jammed packed with department stores, accessories for your every event, apparel for all shapes and sizes, bath, health, and beauty shops to keep you looking your best, cards gifts and books to show your love ones you care, sporting needs to keep you on top of your game, entertainment including all your favorite electronic needs, even eyewear and footwear to boot.

The mall is comprised of three sections: The Plaza, the Court, and the Pavilion. The Plaza being the newest development is located conveniently next to the Court with a footpath connecting the two buildings. Together the Court and Plaza comprise the biggest mall on the East Coast consisting of eight major department stores.

Bloomingdales, JC Penney's, Lord & Taylor, Macy's, Neiman Marcus, Nordstrom, Sears, and Strawbridge's create the exterior of the mall providing entrances into the mall leading to hundreds of stores inside. Whether you're looking for the latest fashion, old- fashion gifts, your everyday needs, practical innovations, or impressive sales the Court and Plaza have everything you need.

Virginia returned home to share her experience with family and friends. This experience was just the beginning for Virginia's adventure of Bundle of Joy. The press releases began. She received calls from radio talk shows about her novel *Til Death Do Us Part: A Marriage Survives the Stress of Military Life.*

This was an era of the scandal of Bill Clinton and Monica Lewinsky and the media was looking for any story that can relate to this scandal. Virginia's novel was an inspiring novel that revealed the challenges of infidelity's claws of destructions. So, the radio talk shows called to listen to Virginia's vision of marital turmoil. One of Bill Clinton's interviews with Oprah revealed Bill Clinton's quote: "Bill Clinton hopes his former paramour, Monica Lewinsky, can someday "have a good life" beyond the scandal ignited by their White House affair. 'I hope that she will not allow her whole life to be defined by her Andy Warhol-like 15 minutes of fame,' Clinton told Oprah Winfrey on her show yesterday."

Clinton described Lewinsky as "a really intelligent person," and said she deserved an apology for the affair and its aftermath. "I think I owed her one and I gave it to her," he said publicly.

Clinton said he has not spoken with Lewinsky since the affair became public and deems it best not to have any contact.

The former President went on to say he hopes "…that the ex-White House intern's life will be full and not solely defined by the fact that she got caught up in this media and political firestorm, because she doesn't deserve that. Nobody does."

If he happened to run into her, Clinton told Winfrey, he would say, hello to her and "I hope you're having a good life."

Lewinsky now lives in the West Village and has dabbled in designing handbags and served as host of a Fox reality series called "Mr. Personality." Her spokeswoman did not return a call for comment yesterday.

Virginia's interview questions were her point of view of the infidelity in marriage and what are the signs of a cheating spouse. Virginia received many interview calls addressing these family issues. This was the beginning of Virginia's celebrity. Carlos couldn't believe the rise of Virginia's fame among the press, but was proud of his wife success, especially if it was bringing positive results among marriage and family unity.

Months had passed, and Junior announced that he will become a father. Junior came home one weekend and announced that Vanessa was pregnant. Virginia and Carlos were shocked. They knew their son was dating, but becoming a father was never revealed. Carlos was speechless and Virginia was in a daze.

"Junior, what do you mean that we will be grandparents in three months? You got to be kidding me."

"No, Dad, I'm not kidding you. I'm going to be a father. Next week we will know the sex of our child."

"So, you are telling me that you all did not use any birth control? You just decided at this point and time in your life that you want to be a father."

"No, but I'm telling you that we were having a sexual relationship and in love and now we are having a baby."

"Virginia, Dear, are you listening to your son?"

"Why, when something goes wrong, you cry... your son. He's our son and, yes, I'm listening. Boy, why did you wait until now to spread the word? You're definitely not giving us any time to plan or do you care?"

"Mom, I knew you and dad would be upset and that's why I put it off. I know you all wanted me to continue going to college, which I'm planning on doing."

"Does Vanessa's parents know that she is pregnant?

And how do they feel about their daughter having a child by an African-American?"

"Mom, yes they know and they are okay with it. I get along with her family."

"Well, there is really nothing for us to say, Junior.

I hope you have prepared yourself for this big responsibility. Being a parent and father is not easy. Yes, we want you to continue in higher education, but if this is what you want and the seed is already planted, the only thing we can do is accept this."

"Junior, you are a grown man and I hope you know what you are getting yourself into. I need some time to adjust and accept this news. I'm going to the garage. You and your mother can talk."

"Mom, dad is mad, isn't he?"

"What do you think? He wanted you to finished college! We both wanted nothing but the best for you. But having a baby is not the end of world, it's a blessing and we will deal with this and support you all the way."

Weeks later, Virginia receives a call from Cynthia in reference to Ms. Steven NAACP annual dinner Banquet. She also told Virginia that one of our members Renee Mullins is the daughter of the deceased James Byrd, and her husband is station back at Fort Riley. Virginia said that she recalled that brutal murder of a black man in Jasper, Texas. Virginia recalled Renee's interview, which read: "Good afternoon. My name is Francis Renee Mullins. I am the oldest daughter of the late Mr. James Byrd Jr. By me being here I feel it provided a foundation for future action. First of all, I would like to thank God for allowing me to be here again for this worthy cause against hate crimes. Last Sunday was my father's 50th birthday. I, my brother Ross, my sister Jamie, and my baby Tayla celebrated it with him at the cemetery. My father loved life and always took the whole month of May to celebrate his day. This month had been the longest month of the year for me and my family.

"As I come before you today it still sends chills through my body just knowing the reasoning behind me being here. I find it difficult to speak today because moments like these let me know, that the fact of the matter is, that my father is gone and has been for almost a year. I feel in my heart I am doing the right thing by supporting this bill, so that no other family will have to suffer my tragic fate. I do not want to sound rhetorical, but I feel as if I have to tell the story in this way. For a moment, I want you to imagine, if you can, walking home from an anniversary party, when three individuals pick you up, take you to a remote area, beat you repeatedly, then while you are still alive chain you by your ankles to the back of a truck and then proceed to drag you for about two and a half to three miles down a logging road. The point in which you actually die after enduring a tremendous amount of pain and broken bones is when your head and arm are ripped from your body like a piece of paper is torn. Now stop imagining. After coming back from the road my dad was dragged to death on, how can we not want to do the right thing and pass this bill? What if it was your father, mother, sister, brother, or even an animal that you love? An animal should not have to undergo what my father went through on the early morning of June 7, 1998.

"This was not just a crime against a 49-year-old African-American that was disabled, but a crime against all humanity. God forbid if it was you. I hope that you would want the people—your fellow citizens—to do something about it and not just sit on their thumbs. I urge this bill to be enacted so my family would at last have some consolation for our anguish. This bill would let me know my dad did not die in vain. To not pass this bill is unfair to police officers and the justice department who work hard to keep people safe. I am here today to be a witness that this, no matter what, cannot be tolerated. It is a very shameful act to be killed because of your race, handicap, gender, or sexual orientation.

I have learned from living 28 years that it takes more energy to hate than to love. As a nation, we must renounce violence and embrace the teachings of nonviolence. My father's untimely death let me know that despite decades of laws, too many people have too little respect for the rights of others, whose only crime is being different. My father's legacy must live on but hate crimes must die.

In closing, remember: Never take life for granted. One minute you are here and the next you are not. Let's not put this bill off and let another innocent victim, like my dad, die by the hands of haters. No law will change the events of June 7th, 1998 but today, nearly a year later, by me being here I hope I can prevent any other acts of violence of this nature from occurring in America. Thank you for allowing me to open my heart to you. May God touch and bless each one of you as we depart.

"This was a very sad tragedy of a love one. Of course, I will be attending Ms. Steven's banquet," commented Virginia.

"Virginia, matter of fact, I think one of Ms. Steven guest speaker is a spokesman for this activist killing held in Jasper. Renee will be one of the honoree guests," said Cynthia.

Virginia and Cynthia attend the NAACP annual banquet. The guest speaker Gary Bledsoe acknowledged Renee Mullins's presence and her activist against hate crimes in Jasper, Texas. Tears begin to flow down Renee's face as the speaker reveals the tragedy of her father's death. The night was memoir for Renee Mullins and the NACCP.

The day has arrived for the birth of the Slaughters first grandchild. The morning of the birth of their grandchild, Carlos and Virginia was getting dressed for work when they received a call from Vanessa's parents informing them that she had given birth to a boy. Carlos answered the phone and passed the phone to Virginia as he was leaving for work. Vanessa's mother, Carol, revealed that it's a boy weighing seven pounds and five ounces. Virginia was excited. She asked had they contacted Junior. Carol said that Vanessa called and Junior was on his way home. Virginia told her that she will call in and let her supervisor know that she will not be in due to the birth of her grandson. Virginia called Carlene in Overland, Kansas, announcing the birth of their grandson and her nephew. Carlene was full of joy and said that she will be home to see her nephew. Virginia, full of joy, went shopping for Vanessa's gift to take to the hospital. Virginia arrived at the hospital nursing station announcing that she's the proud grandparent of Vanessa's "bundle of joy." Vanessa introduced her parents, Carol and John. Virginia showered Vanessa with presents. Vanessa said that we were going to have the baby shower in two weeks, but now they are going to have to wait. Virginia said that they still can have the shower and the guest will know exactly what to purchase—gifts for a boy. Virginia asked where the baby was. Carol said they will be bringing him in a few minutes.

"Vanessa had the baby in this room. Yep, they don't have a delivery room anymore. They had curtains pulled and we saw the entire delivery procedures. We thought that it will be hours, but soon as we arrived and they began to prep, Vanessa screamed the baby is coming and out came our little boy. He's so cute."

Just when Virginia was about to ask how long it will be, the nurse came in the room with their bundle of joy. The nurse placed the baby in Vanessa's arms.

"You can give him to his grandmother," Vanessa said.

"Are you sure? I can wait," Virginia said.

"Yes, I'm sure. I'll have plenty of time to hold him."

The nurse placed the baby boy in Virginia's arms.

"He looks just like his dad when he was born. I must agree with your other grandma, you are a handsome boy." Virginia hears a noise and it was Carlos entering the room. Carlos walked toward Virginia and his grandson. Carol and John introduced themselves.

"Nice to meet you," said Carlos. "So, this is the baby boy?"

"This is our grandson, Carlos. Here, do you want to hold him?"

"Wait a minute, let me get myself together. It's been a long time since I held a baby."

"Hold your hand out and I'll place him in your arms."

"He's kind of heavy. How much did he weigh?"

"He weighed seven pounds and five ounces."

"That's the same as Junior weighed when he was born."

"The nurse said he has a big head," said Vanessa. "I told her that he must have gotten that from his dad."

"Yep, that's the Slaughters' trademark, a big head, but he's a cute little boy."

Both families were enjoying the birth of their first grandchild. Junior arrives at Geary County Community Hospital from Kansas City. He entered the Maternity Ward, identified himself, and the nurse directed him to Vanessa's room.

"Junior should be arriving anytime. Knowing my son, he will come straight to the hospital," remarked Virginia.

Minutes later, Junior entered the room.

Junior went and kiss Vanessa and his mother. "Dad I see you already getting used to being a granddad. You already got your hands full."

"Yep, we were just saying how much he looked like you when you were born. Here, you can hold your son. Yeah, now you are going to see what it feels like being in my shoes, when he starts wearing those hundred dollars sneakers and don't want to hear he don't need that. Payback is something else. God is good all the time," Carlos said.

"Dad, you are right."

"Junior, how does it feel being a father?" Virginia asked.

"Mom, it feels good and I'm definitely going to do right by my son. He's not going to want for nothing just like my parents provided for me. Hey, I got the cigar."

"Yep, that's right… we got to pass them out. Even if I don't smoke, I want my cigar. I don't have to light it."

"Have you all picked out the baby's name?" Virginia asked.

"Yep, he's going to be named after his grandfathers and father. He got a long name, but we are going to call him CJ."

"That's right keeping it simple."

Virginia walked to a corner in the room admiring Carlos and Junior as they gaze at CJ. Virginia could see the joy in both their faces. History has finally begun to repeat itself. The birth of their grandchild was the beginning of the bi-racial generations, but this time, it will be different. History will be written, accepted, and acknowledged with love, joy, and happiness in unity.

Months passed, and the birth of the Slaughters' grandchild was the beginning of a new era. CJ brought joy and happiness to the family. Virginia would often find herself in a daze as she watched the bonding of a father and a grandfather bonding with CJ. During the Christmas holiday seasons over the years, CJ was the center of attention. Opening presents brings lots of laughter among the family gather. Carlos spent a lot of time teaching his grandson sports, hunting, and fishing. The Slaughters planned their vacations, taking their grandson to amusement parks and shopping. Carlos didn't have the opportunity to spend time with Junior, but CJ brought joy to Carlos bestowing him with the opportunity to capture those precious moments he lost with his son due to his career. He shared with his grandson his active duty years as a soldier, and at one time, in CJ's younger years he had a great desire to become a soldier just like his grandfather, but the continuous drill of soldiering through the eyes of Carlos had brought a halt of change for CJ. But can one is to tell, CJ just might recapture his desire as he got older.

CHAPTER ELEVEN

UNFOLDING DREAMS

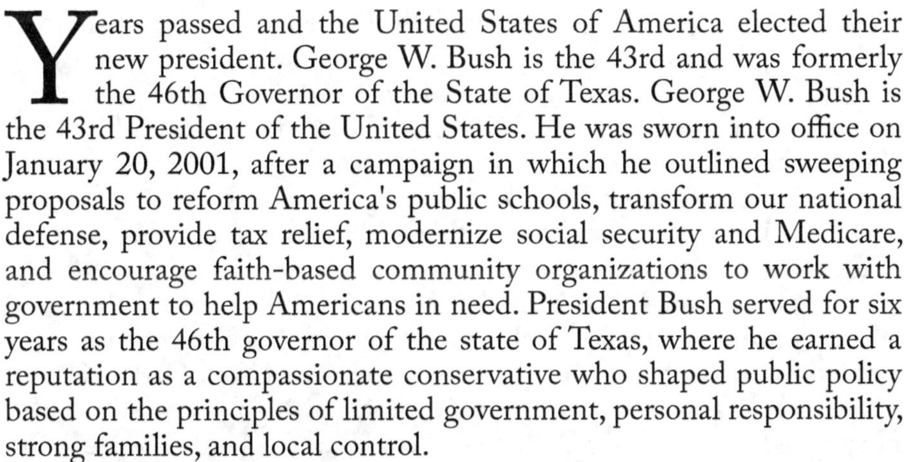

Years passed and the United States of America elected their new president. George W. Bush is the 43rd and was formerly the 46th Governor of the State of Texas. George W. Bush is the 43rd President of the United States. He was sworn into office on January 20, 2001, after a campaign in which he outlined sweeping proposals to reform America's public schools, transform our national defense, provide tax relief, modernize social security and Medicare, and encourage faith-based community organizations to work with government to help Americans in need. President Bush served for six years as the 46th governor of the state of Texas, where he earned a reputation as a compassionate conservative who shaped public policy based on the principles of limited government, personal responsibility, strong families, and local control.

President Bush was born on July 6, 1946, in New Haven, Connecticut, and he grew up in Midland and Houston, Texas. He received a bachelor's degree from Yale University in 1968, and then served as an F-102 fighter pilot in the Texas Air National Guard. President Bush received a Master of Business Administration from Harvard Business School in 1975. After graduating, he moved back to Midland and began a career in the energy business. After working on his father's successful 1988 presidential campaign, he assembled the group of partners that purchased the Texas Rangers baseball franchise in 1989.

He served as managing general partner of the Texas Rangers until he was elected Governor on November 8, 1994, with 53.5 percent of the vote. He became the first governor in Texas history to be elected to consecutive four-year terms when he was re-elected on November 3, 1998 with 68.6 percent of the vote.

Since taking office, President Bush signed into law bold initiatives to improve public schools by raising standards, requiring accountability, and strengthening local control. He signed tax relief that provided rebate checks and lower tax rates for everyone who pays income taxes in America. He has increased pay and benefits for America's military and is working to save and strengthen social security and Medicare. He is also committed to ushering in a responsibility era in America and has called on all Americans to be "…citizens, not spectators; citizens, not subjects; responsible citizens building communities of service and a nation of character." This was the beginning of a new era—an era of war.

On the morning of September 11, 2001, Virginia and Carlos went to work as usually assuming to have another normal day. They had received a call early that morning from Carlene saying that she was flying to California for a conference. But on this particular morning, a tragedy happened that the world changed forever. Virginia was preparing to conduct her briefing when Mr. Moon announced that the World Trade Center had been hit by airplanes. Virginia was startled and couldn't believe what she was hearing.

"Virginia, I can't believe it either," Mr. Moon said. "But they say that it's on the news."

Virginia immediately turned on her radio and listened to the news, which confirmed the World Trade Center had been bombed and all airports are on alert. Virginia began to panic and called Carlos. Carlos said that he was aware of the bombing and waiting for Carlene to call. He assured Virginia that Carlene will call once she landed because she knows that they will be worried and Carlene always called. They both agreed to call each other once they hear from Carlene. Meanwhile, Virginia resumed preparing for her briefing. Mr. Moon overheard Virginia's conversations and assigned someone else to conduct the briefing, instructing Virginia to calm down and assuring her that everything will be okay. The office was crazy that morning, everyone stood by and listened to the news. Finally, Virginia's phone rang, it was Carlos calling saying that Carlene just called and has landed safely in California, and the airport was flooding with security. Virginia was relieved to hear this news. Everyone returned to their work stations receiving email photos of the explosions. Minutes later, Sgt. Osuma came walking in the office, revealing another airplane explosion Flight

77 has hit the Pentagon and some of the friends of PSB soldiers and colleague had been killed.

The next day, Fort Riley, became a closed post with guard stations at all entrance. This tragedy changed Fort Riley and other open military installation for all times.

The attacks of September 11th changed America—and in President Bush's words, "...in our grief and anger, we have found our mission and our moment." President Bush declared war against terror and has made victory in the war on terrorism, and the advancement of human freedom became the priority of his administration. Already, the United States military and a great coalition of nations have liberated the people of Afghanistan from the brutal Taliban regime and denied al Qaeda its safe haven of operations. Thousands of terrorists were captured or killed and operations were disrupted in many countries around the world. In the president's words, "...our nation—this generation—will lift a dark threat of violence from our people and our future. We will rally the world to this cause by our efforts, by our courage. We will not tire, we will not falter, and we will not fail."

Months later, Virginia had a book signing in Macon, in Barnes & Noble bookstore and an interview with Carol Minn on their midday show on channel 13. Carlene decided to travel with her mother since Carlos couldn't attend. They did not want Virginia traveling alone. Even, though the war on terrorism shocked the nation, the American people refused to live in fear. Virginia flew from Kansas Airport for the first time since the war on terrorism began. The vision of change at the airport had heavy security guards checking in passengers and their baggage, which took, on average, 90 minutes processing time. Never in a million years did Virginia imagine the day that she would be exposed to personal security, checking her purse, clothing, shoes, and more. Airports under alert posted signs everywhere.

This was very frustrating to the American people who lived in freedom for many years without the threat of terrorism. American lifestyle suddenly changed due to evil and anger revenge of Saddam Hussein's coalition. The Bush administration was determined to attack Iraq and capture Saddam Hussein dead or alive. The president's intentions were to free the Iraqis from the power of the Hussein's coalition and the only way to accomplish this mission was to declare war on Iraq.

Virginia's flight arrived safely. Family and friends attended the book signing and were tuned in to channel 13 to watch the interview. Virginia and Tricia were out shopping when they ran into Teddy's aunt Lorena who told them of Teddy's leukemia. Virginia was shocked. Aunt Lorena said that Teddy and his family were visiting from Germany due to his illness and invited Virginia to come by the house for a visit.

"It had been years since Teddy last saw you," Aunt Lorena remarked. "We saw the interview on channel 13. His mother called Mrs. Slaughter to get an autographed copy of your novels."

"My sister retrieved the message from the answer machine. Let them know that I got their message," Virginia said.

"Virginia, you know we have not had time to check the phone messages," Tricia said.

"I know, we have been ripping and running all day. I did not want to tell Lorena because of her sad facial expression. Teddy must be very ill."

Tricia and Virginia return home and shared their news with Carlene and Shawn. Minutes later, there was a knock at the door, it was cousin Debra stopping by to congratulate Virginia on her interview. Debra came in, hugged Virginia and Carlene, and sat on the couch. Tricia, Carlene, and Shawn left to go get something to eat while Debra chatted with Virginia.

"I got a copy of your novel," Debra said. "Now, am I in your second book?"

"Now, Debra, when have I left you out of my novels?

I know how much you love being a character."

"Yep, and if your novel becomes a film, don't forget I want to play my own character. No one can act the part but the real Debra."

"Girl, you haven't changed a bit. Did you know that Teddy and his family are in town?"

"No, I didn't know that!"

"That's right, we ran into Lorena and she told us that he has leukemia and apparently is very sick, judging from her tone of voice and facial expressions."

"Virginia, what are you doing? Let's go over to his aunt's house. I know the location. You know you want to see for yourself. I know I want too."

"Well, I don't know if I should go."

"Why not? It's nothing wrong seeing a long-lost friend. Besides, he could be dying."

"I guess you are right. let's head out!"

Debra drove Virginia to Aunt Lorena's house. The girls prepared themselves for the worst.

"I hope he is not connected to tubes. This is sad. I don't see any cars. Oh, Lorena's car is park on the street."

"Hold up, Debra. Let me get myself together. Girl, I never expected to see him ill after all these years. I wonder what his wife looks like."

"Well, we are going to see!"

The girls walked to the front door and Debra rang the doorbell.

"Hi, Debra and Virginia. I see you both came by and I gather you all want to see Teddy. Come in and have a seat!"

The ladies entered the house and were escorted to the living room while Lorena went to get Teddy. They both sat, Debra in the loveseat and Virginia on the couch.

"He must not be that ill since we were not escorted to the bedroom. I guest he can walk," Debra said.

"Don't talk too loud. You know they can hear us!"

"Girl, who cares? They know we probably are wondering how bad he is looking!"

Minutes later, Teddy entered the living room. Teddy grabbed Debra and embraced. Then he slowly went to the couch, glancing at Virginia and gave her a hug.

"Debra, it's been years since I've seen you."

"Yep, it's been about 26 years or more."

"So, what have you being doing? Are you still married? The last I heard you had three boys!"

"Where you get that from? I only have two!"

"Oh. I'm sorry. I must have got the info wrong!"

Teddy and Debra continued to update about their family. Virginia sat on the couch listening to their conversation. Teddy finally got around engaging in conversation with Virginia.

"Looking good with a smile. Virginia, you have not changed much in over 26 years since we last saw each other. You had married Slaughter when we last spoke. I have been hearing a lot about you and, every time I hear about you, they say you still looking good, and now I can definitely comment on that!"

"Well, I don't know about all that, but I do try to hold myself together. I have gained some weight over the years due to age and bearing children."

"Hey, Virginia. You still looked good. We all age, gain weight, but you are carrying it well. Stand up and let me take another look at you."

"I'm not going to stand up so you can see the extra weight."

"No, stand up. I saw your interview and girl you were great and looking good as usual. The extra weight becomes you. That's okay, you will stand up when you leave."

"Now, tell me what's going on with you. You don't appear to be sick."

"Yep, I'm having problems finding a matching donor.

It's complicated and I don't want to spend our time discussing my illness. I've had it for years and I'm on medication and doing fine. Let me introduce you to my wife and daughter." Teddy leaves to get his wife and daughter.

"I didn't think they were here the way, he was talking and drooling at the mouth looking at you. Girl, he still got a thing for you," Debra said.

"Hush. I hear them coming up the hallway!"

"Virginia and Debra, I want to introduce to my wife, Greta, and my daughter Cassandra. My son did not come with us. He graduates this year and is going to enlist in the German armed forces."

"It's nice to meet you," Greta said. "I see you both are staring. Yes, I'm much older than Teddy."

"I'm sorry, I didn't mean to stare," Virginia said. "But your age did cross my mind!"

"Well... I'm not going to stay. It was nice meeting the both of you!"

"Hey, Cassandra, come and sit by me. Now, how old are you?" Virginia asked.

"I'm ten, going on eleven years old."

"Well, you are a pretty little girl and I can see that you are very excited about becoming eleven years old."

"I will be eleven May 13 of next year."

Virginia continued to chat with Cassandra. Teddy continued to gaze at Virginia. It was getting late and Virginia told Debra it was time for them leave and said she had enjoyed their visit. Lorena enters the living room and extended her thanks for their visit, and Teddy escorted the ladies to their car. Virginia insisted that he did not have to escort them, but Teddy refused to listen and did it anyway. He escorted Virginia all the way, opened the door, and asked where they were headed. Virginia immediately said home and Debra concurred.

"Debra, can't I get you and Virginia to meet me somewhere later?" Teddy asked.

"I'm going home. That's between you and Virginia."

"Girl, you still haven't changed. Virginia, I just can't believe my eyes. How good you looked."

Virginia rolled up the car window. "Okay, Teddy. I'll see you and you take care of yourself. Bye!"

Teddy was still holding on not wanting to release the door waved good-bye. Debra and Virginia pulled out of Lorena's driveway. Teddy stayed standing in the driveway watching the ladies as they drive down the street.

"Girl, Teddy still has feelings for you. I bet he hated every day you and him broke up. You can see it in his eyes."

"What do you mean see it in his eyes? He is a married man."

"That doesn't matter. Did you take a good look at his wife? She looks bad."

"Yep, she does look old. I wonder where he met her. Oh, yeah, I forgot he was in the military during the same time we were stationed in Germany; Carlos first tour."

"Now, tell me and be honest, you still don't think about the old days when you and Teddy were together? We just knew you all would marry."

"Debra, we thought we would marry, too. Matter of fact, we discussed our future: planning a family, career, and the works, but we just couldn't make it. You know Teddy loves his women and I just could not handle that anymore and, no, I don't have deep feelings for

Teddy, only friendship. He didn't look sickly to me. His aunt lied to get me to come over to see him."

"Yeah, he didn't look sick to me. He looked good to have leukemia, don't you think?"

"Yeah, he does look good!"

"See, I got you!"

"No, I don't mean it like that!"

"I'm just teasing you, but it sure would have been nice if you all had married, then you will be living here in Macon."

"Well, it's too late to dwell on what might have happened. I'm glad to see that he's not as bad as I assumed."

Debra dropped Virginia home and Virginia told Tricia and Carlene where they had gone. Carlene was upset she didn't get the opportunity to meet Teddy. Virginia told Tricia that she promised Teddy that she will give an autograph copy of her novels to his mother because he will be flying out tomorrow returning to Germany. Carlene insisted that she will be going with them when they visit his mother. The next day, Carlene got the opportunity to meet Teddy's mother and saw photos of her mother's childhood sweetheart. She complimented his looks, hospitality, and elegant home during their visit. Carlene was glad to finally see the environment of her mother's childhood sweetheart, saying her mother does have good taste in men, but she was glad she married her dad; otherwise, she would not be here.

Carlene and Virginia returned home. Two months later, Virginia began her debut hosting and producing her radio talk show. It was a success, blossoming nationwide. "On the Air." This was a dream Virginia never desired but unfolded and was very successful.

During this time of success for Virginia, Junior landed a job with one of the wealthiest companies in the state of Kansas as a loan consultant. Unfolding Dreams were blossoming throughout the Slaughter family.

CHAPTER TWELVE

CLOSE ENCOUNTERS

A year passed and it was 2003, the war on terror was still an active mission. The reservists continued to be called up to assist in the war, and the word went that retirees would soon be called back for active duty. Carlos and Virginia were enjoying their happy life of marriage and as grandparents. Virginia observed the yearning and loving bond of her grandson and his grandpa Carlos. They often spent time planning vacations with their grandson. The time came for Carlos to plan a Thanksgiving in Macon. For years, the Slaughters spent their Thanksgivings at their home where Virginia and Carlos prepared the dinner, slaving in the kitchen. But this season, Carlos decided that he will celebrate with family in Macon and relieve Virginia and himself from preparing the festivities. Friends and family were sad to hear that the Slaughters will not be opening their home to celebrate the feast with their soul food.

Carlos fried Turkey and Virginia made deserts, side dishes, collard greens, homemade macaroni and cheese, potato salads, and sweet potatoes. Carlene and Junior could not believe that their parents were not cooking. This is the first time they will not be celebrating the holidays in their parents' home and decided to join them in Macon.

The Slaughters flew to Georgia and CJ went with them, who never miss a vacation trip. They arrived at Atlanta Airport, got a rental car, and drove to Macon, Georgia. Carlos did not tell his mother of his arrival date. They pulled in on Mrs. Slaughter's driveway, and Carlos knocked on the door. Mrs. Slaughter, in tears, embraced her son and family. Of course, Grandma Slaughter had many questions and was glad to see them. This was a grand reunion for the Cottingham and

Slaughters who joined together to spend their holidays eating Grandma Slaughter's good old soul food. The event was held aunt Anna Mae's house. Kirk traveled down from Atlanta and announced he was on assignment to Okinawa, Japan. He secretly mentioned to Carlos that he may be going to Iraq once he stayed in Okinawa for three months. The festivities included eating, dancing, and playing cards. Grandma Slaughter and sisters gathered on the floor doing the Electra Slide and R Kelly song "Step in Name of Love," a new release. The week event among friends and family was one they will never forget.

They returned home and Virginia was ripping and running planning the Annual New Year Ball Event. This event was sponsored by the Daughter of Isis, which Virginia was the chairman of. Virginia's committee was busy and Cynthia once again supported her all the way. Virginia spread the word of this event by radio, television and the *Daily Union* newspaper. Tickets were on sale throughout the store in Junction City and Manhattan where the event will be held at the Ramada Inn. This was Virginia's second year as chairman of the event, as usual, hoping for another successful ball.

The ball was held and the Slaughters once again had a wonderful time mingling among friends ringing in the New Year 2004. Fort Riley's vision of change of closed post changed the lifestyle for many soldiers who enjoyed leaving the post to celebrate this event. But for many soldiers, they had celebrated on post due to fear of DUIs and security check returning on post. For many events the numbers were low in quantity of soldier participation throughout the civilian community holiday's events.

Two months later, Virginia was preparing for her radio talk show. She received a call from Cynthia about a meeting in Manhattan. She wanted to know did she receive the email about getting a bus to travel to the Imperial Conference. Virginia confirmed receipt of the email and told Cynthia that she will see her at the meeting.

The next day, Virginia dressed for the meeting. Carlos up and dressed, kissed Virginia saying that he was taking photos at the Nobles meeting and will see her there because their meeting was starting early. Virginia was getting mixed feelings about going to the meeting. She received a call from Daughter Joyce confirming her attendance. Virginia confirmed that she was getting ready to leave.

On the morning of February 21, 2004, Virginia departed her home for Manhattan, Kansas. Virginia drove from her driveway heading for I-70 taking the exit for K-18 or Fort Riley Boulevard. Once she entered K-18, driving in the far-left lane and approaching 52nd Ave, Virginia noticed a red pickup truck entering K-18 failing to yield to the right lane traffic. She immediately began to reduce her speed and continued to noticed the truck crossing, driving across her lane. Virginia's thought quickly and decided that the only way to avoid a head on collision, she must make a quick left turn going in the direction of the red truck. Virginia focused on the traveling truck, made the left turn, screamed, and crashing into the red truck.

Meanwhile, traffic was slowing down and a white gentleman quickly pulled over to assist Virginia. Virginia was knocked unconscious, when she came back she was coughing due to the exploded airbag hitting her in her face. She immediately tried to release her seatbelt as the gentlemen opened her car. One of them yelled, "Are you alright? We've got to get you out of this car. Your vehicle is leaking and we don't know if there is going to be an explosion."

"Mam, can you move?" one gentleman asked. "I got you, just help me remove you from the car."

Virginia faintly saw and heard the gentlemen trying to release her seatbelt to get her out of the car, she felt pain in her left leg.

"Can you walk? You can lean on me. We got to get you across the street." The gentleman gets Virginia across the street. Virginia screamed to get her purse. Please will someone get my purse from the front seat? The gentlemen get someone to monitor Virginia while he goes to retrieve Virginia's purse. Minutes later, Virginia heard a voice she recognizes, it's Barbara, the lady who used to work at Burger King at Fort Riley. She told Barbara to please get her cellphone from her purse and call Carlos. There was no answer from Carlos's number. The gentleman continuously trying to keep Virginia awake was holding her head upward yelling for an ambulance. Barbara knelt down to Virginia, saying there was no answer, and Virginia told her to select Cynthia's name. Barbara reached Cynthia and told her of the accident, saying that the ambulance was on its way and for her to meet them at Manhattan Regional Health Hospital. Virginia passed out. The gentlemen yelled about the ambulance and Barbara said she can see them coming. The ambulance arrives and provides medical assistance to Virginia. The gentleman, having no knowledge of Virginia's injuries, provided excellent assistance. The medical technicians strapped Virginia to the board and loaded her into their vehicle. They continued to give medical treatment as the ambulance drove to the hospital.

Meanwhile at the Douglas Center, Maria came entering the meeting room yelling if Virginia was there. Cynthia told Maria to calm down and asked what was wrong. Maria said that there was a terrible accident on K-18 and the vehicle looked like Virginia's car. Cynthia's phones rang and it was Barbara calling about Virginia's accident. Cynthia provides the members of Virginia's accident and rush out to fetch Carlos. Cynthia entered the Nobles building and told Carlos that Virginia had been in an accident. Carlos immediately set up his equipment while Cynthia told her husband to be responsible of getting Carlos's equipment. Carlos nervously held back tears and yelled for Cynthia to hurry up. They rushed to Carlos's truck and they raced to the hospital.

"What happened?" Carlos asked. "I thought she was at the meeting?"

"Carlos, I don't know. All I know is Barbara call and she said they were taking Virginia to the hospital. She didn't know the extent of Virginia's injuries."

"Cynthia you better fasten your seatbelt because this is going to be one hell of a ride."

They arrived at the hospital before the ambulance. Cynthia told the nurse that Carlos was the patient's husband and he's very upset, asking them not to stop them from entering and asked if the ambulance arrived.

The ambulance finally arrived and transferred Virginia to an emergency room bed. In tremendous fear, Carlos pushed his way into the emergency room. Upon seeing Virginia, with tears in his eyes, he yelled, "What up sexy? Are you alright?"

Virginia heard Carlos's voice and tried to response. She slowly cried out, "Carlos, please don't leave me!"

"Sexy, I'm going to be right here."

"Where is Cynthia?"

"She is right here, too. I'm sending a nurse to get her."

The Nurse retrieved Cynthia from the waiting room and escorted her to Virginia's bedside. Virginia heard Cynthia's voice and thanked her for being by her side in a moment of distress. The doctors continued providing treatment to Virginia and announced the family and friends that they must take Virginia to the radiologist. Carlos immediately went to Virginia's bed, in tears, kissing her, saying I'm will be right here when you return, assuring Virginia that she will be fine. Cynthia and Carlos paced the lobby floor waiting for Virginia to return.

"Man, this is a very close encounter. God is good all the time. Cynthia, it's going to be on, when I take her home, but that's alright, because I just don't know what I will do without my baby."

"Yep you know that you got to be on it. Virginia is going to want a lot of attention."

"Oh, I know, she can ask for anything, and I will be right there waiting on her."

Virginia returned from x-ray and the nurse took her vital signs. Carlos and Cynthia were observing while Virginia constantly babbled about the accident tragedy. The doctors decided to keep Virginia overnight for observation. Cynthia and Carlos took turns sitting with her. He decided not to mention anything to the kids at this time. The next day, Virginia's vital signs reading were back to normal and the doctors released her from the hospital.

Virginia returned home and was settled into her bedroom. While Cynthia settled Virginia in her bed, Carlos phoned family and friends about the accident. Mrs. Slaughter told Carlos that Teddy passed away yesterday. She told her son that the funeral services will be announced once the body had been flown back to the United States. Carlos told Virginia of this sad news. Virginia phoned Tricia to ensure that Teddy's family is sent flowers. That following week, Virginia attended her first appointment with Dr. Mace who referred Virginia to Geary County Rehabilitation Center. Virginia was very weak and could barely walk into the building. The reception directed the Slaughters to an examination room. The facility director Ann entered Virginia's room for an initial briefing. Minutes later, Ann assigned Virginia to Amy for physical therapy. Virginia didn't complain about the treatment. Ann ensured the family that Virginia will recover from this accident showing the family photos on the wall of successful patient recovery. Virginia looked at the picture and image of the girl in the photo bending down touching her toes.

During the night, while Virginia was sleeping, she had a dream about her mother dressed in the gown she was buried in, standing at the foot of her bed. It appeared that Mrs. Cottingham was assuring her daughter that Carlos will provide support and in time, her wounds will heal. Virginia tried to reach out and embrace her mother, but Mrs. Cottingham began to fade away in the bright shining light. Virginia struggled to wake up from the dream but is held bound into a deep sleep. Virginia finally woke up and shared her dream with Carlos.

Carlos was very concern about his wife recovery. There were days when Virginia's pain was very severe, until he noticed a change in her attitude of giving up on hope for a successful recovery. Carlos constantly presented individuals whose illnesses were worse than Virginia how these individual clung for hope. Virginia was in a lot of pain for several weeks, but with Carlos's support and encouragement, Virginia regained her faith. Virginia refused to give up the thought of not walking. She was determined to fight this illness, thanks to Carlos's support. The kids would call and visit periodically.

Months later, the news said gays were granted the right to marry in the state of California. This news was devastating for many Americans who are against same sex marriage, but in recent months, however, some activist judges and local officials have made an aggressive attempt to redefine marriage. In Massachusetts, four judges on the highest court have indicated they will order the issuance of marriage licenses to applicants of the same gender on May of this year. In San Francisco, city officials have issued thousands of marriage licenses to people of the same gender, contrary to the California family code. That code, which clearly defined marriage as the union of a man and a woman, was approved overwhelmingly by the voters of California. A county in New Mexico had also issued marriage licenses to applicants of the same gender. And unless action was taken, we can expect more arbitrary court decisions, more litigation, more defiance of the law by local officials, all of which added to uncertainty.

After more than two centuries of American jurisprudence, and millennia of human experience, a few judges and local authorities are presuming to change the most fundamental institution of civilization. Their actions have created confusion on an issue that required clarity.

On a matter of such importance, the voice of the people must be heard. Activist courts have left the people with recourse. If we are to prevent the meaning of marriage from being changed forever, our nation must enact a constitutional amendment to protect marriage in America. Decisive and democratic action was needed, because attempts to redefine marriage in a single state or city could have serious consequences throughout the country.

The Constitution says that full faith and credit shall be given in each state to the public acts and records and judicial proceedings of every other state. Those who wanted to change the meaning of marriage will claim that this provision required all states and cities to recognize same-sex marriages performed anywhere in America. Congress attempted to address this problem in the Defense of Marriage Act, by declaring that no state must accept another state's definition of marriage. My administration will vigorously defend this act from congress.

Yet there is no assurance that the Defense of Marriage Act will not, itself, be struck down by activist courts. In that event, every state would be forced to recognize any relationship that judges in Boston or officials in San Francisco choose to call a marriage. Furthermore, even if the Defense of Marriage Act was upheld, the law does not protect marriage within any state or city.

For all these reasons, the Defense of Marriage requires a constitutional amendment. An amendment to the Constitution was never to be undertaken lightly. The amendment process has addressed many serious matters of national concern. And the preservation of marriage has risen to this level of national importance. The union of a man and woman was the most enduring human institution, honoring—honored and encouraged in all cultures and by every religious faith. Ages of experience have taught humanity that the commitment of a husband and wife to love and to serve one another promotes the welfare of children and the stability of society.

Marriage cannot be severed from its cultural, religious and natural roots without weakening the good influence of society. Government, by recognizing and protecting marriage, serves the interests of all. Today, I call upon the congress to promptly pass, and to send to the states for ratification, an amendment to our constitution defining and protecting marriage as a union of man and woman as husband and wife. The amendment should fully protect marriage while leaving the state legislatures free to make their own choices in defining legal arrangements other than marriage.

America is a free society, which limits the role of government in the lives of our citizens. This commitment of freedom, however, does not require the redefinition of one of our most basic social institutions. Our government should respect every person and protect the institution of marriage. There is no contradiction between these responsibilities. We should also conduct this difficult debate in a manner worthy of our country, without bitterness or anger.

Two months had passed, Virginia's body was finally responding to the therapy. She still was having the pain in her lower back and leg, but her body was conditioned to adjust to the pain. Virginia had a doctor's appointment and decided she wanted to return to work on half-day schedule and continue her therapy. Dr. Mace agreed providing a work order of limited duties, due to Virginia's injures reminding Virginia of the importance of light duties and not to take any chances of going beyond her restrictions order. The doctor told Virginia it will take at least six months or more before any relief of severe pain saying that it is damage to the spine—bulging disk—that will heal in time. How long, no one knows because each body is different, but due to age, Virginia's illness will take longer. The doctor indicated that she probably will have to administer pain injections for relief, but for now, she has referred Virginia to Geary County Rehab Center.

Veronica and Anita would call Virginia weekly to check on her recovery. Veronica would call expressing her wisdom of home remedy treatment. Virginia was glad to hear from her friendly colleagues. They would always keep in touch before and after the moments of distress. Veronica's son was graduating and she invited Virginia and Carlos to the graduation. Virginia's health would not allow her to attend Veronica son's graduation, but she did attend his reception at Veronica's house with the ravishing soul food and delicious treats. The ladies reminisced their days at Irwin Army Community Hospital when they worked together in fun and laughter to rise above their stressful encounters.

Weeks later in news, Virginia and Carlos was watching coverage on CNN the announcement of the nation 40th president's death. Former President Ronald Reagan died Saturday at his home in Los Angeles. He was 93. Reagan led a conservative revolution that set the economic and cultural tone of the 1980s hastened the end of the Cold War and revitalized the Republican Party. He suffered from Alzheimer's disease since at least late 1994. At 69, Reagan was the oldest man elected president when he was chosen on November 4, 1980, over incumbent Democrat Jimmy Carter.

On March 30, 1981, Reagan was leaving a Washington hotel after addressing labor leaders when John Hinckley fired six gunshots at him. A bullet lodged an inch from Reagan's heart, but he recovered fully.

In 1984, he defeated Democrat Walter Mondale. He is known the fallen of the Iron Curtain that separated East and West Berlin. President Reagan had said, "We will always remember. We will always be proud. We will always be prepared, so we will always be free."

The time had arrived for the Juneteenth celebration held in Manhattan, Kansas. Virginia received a call inviting Virginia to attend the Daughters meeting. Virginia told Joyce that she would attend the meeting. The morning of the meeting, Carlos was very reluctant about his wife's driving to Manhattan traveling on K-18, the road where her accident occurred. Virginia told Carlos that he cannot live in fear every time she travels to Manhattan, she assured Carlos that besides, she has not prevailed the memory of that horrible accident and will take I-70 and exit 313 to Manhattan. Carlos kisses his wife and reminded Virginia to turn on her cellphone and call when she arrives in Manhattan. Carlos listened fearfully to the call from Virginia announcing her safe arrival, while driving to CJ's T-Ball game.

Carlos arrived at the game and CJ asked where "nana" was. Carlos informed CJ that nana had to attend a meeting and she could not attend his game that day, a second later, the phone rang, Carlos's heart relaxed, and gave CJ the phone. Virginia wished CJ the best of luck during his game and apologized for not being there but assured him that she will be at his next game.

"That's, okay Nana," said CJ. "I'm just glad that you are feeling better. Papa is here to cheer for the both of you… love you!" CJ returned the phone to Carlos and he said, "I love you and drive safely," hanging up the phone. That day was the beginning of freedom for both Virginia and Carlos of letting go, allowing Virginia to return to freedom of independence and driving without fear.

Virginia was glad to be among her auxiliary members, functioning mental and physical performance expressing her ideas. Joyce knew that Virginia's health was not at full recovery but encouraged Virginia to attend the Juneteenth event assisting with collecting money. Virginia agreed indicating that she has no idea from day to day how her health condition will be until she wakes up and gets going. Joyce understood and reminded Virginia to have faith and she will have an inspirational day on Juneteenth.

Juneteenth was the oldest known celebration of the ending of slavery. From its origin at Galveston, Texas, in 1865, the observance of June 19th as the African-American Emancipation Day had spread across the United States and beyond.

Virginia scheduled a hair appointment at Design Creations with Pamela. It has been a very long time since Virginia had been to Design Creations. Pamela updated Virginia on her lifestyle changes saying that her husband will be returning from Iraq among the troop cycle rotation in Fort Riley. Pamela said that she had received a copy of her husband's extension orders and was afraid to mention it to him on the phone. Pamela continued to mention how one of her husband's colleagues had returned and in unit formation, when the soldier returned from Iraq, the soldier stepped out of formation, in anger and ran grabbing his wife bounding away at her. The commander released the soldiers from formation, as some had already stepped out from formation to provide assistance to the soldier and his wife. The soldiers immediately pulled away and held out his hands for arrest. Pamela mentioned this to her husband about what had happened in his unit and he revealed that his colleague was upset with his spouse due to a $20,000 debt the spouse occurred during the soldier's absence. This news saddened Virginia's heart because there were many soldiers who have risked their life for their families' improvement of lifestyle and what do they receive upon their return, domestic turmoil of infidelity, financial issues, news of continuous deployment, etc. Pamela mentioned how she increased her family's saving account, paid off bills and decorated their home. She said that it was rough not having that support caring for her children and managing her salon business, but her dedication to her family pulled her through. Virginia was proud to hear that Pamela focused on their family needs and the improvement of their lifestyle, so when her spouse returned from the warzone, his tour will not be in vain, but proudly serving a better future for his family and the nations freedom. Virginia assured Pamela that her husband will receive his copy of the extension of his assignment before he departs Iraq. The ladies continued to chat about Virginia's illness and recovery.

Across the nation, homeland security was high priority. Terrorism threat continued to increase as presidential elections candidates expressed their concern among other issues. Fort Riley's vision of change emerged with civilian guards posting on the gate entrance. Bill Clinton is in the news announcing his novel *My Life*. Virginia received a call from Carlene announcing Bill Clinton visiting University of Kansas. Carlene mentioned how she stood in line for hours to get her ticket to this event.

The Juneteenth event celebration had arrived and Virginia attended this great event. Their organization sold Funnel Cakes, water, polish sausages, and sodas. The day was very cloudy and cold. Virginia's body began to ache with pain and Cynthia suggested that Virginia return home, but Virginia decided to go inside the lodge's warm building. Minutes later, Virginia returned to the auxiliary tent and the sun began to shine and temperature began to rise. The day turned out to be a great day and a successful event for everyone.

During this era in news, the death of a great artist of music Ray Charles died. The Universal Pictures movie *Ray* (formerly titled *Unchain My Heart: The Ray Charles Story*) is a tribute to Charles's life and legacy. Jamie Foxx portrayed Charles in the film. The time arrived for the Slaughters to travel to Macon to attend the Slaughters' family reunion. Cousin Cheryl called Virginia weeks before the event to inquire about Carlene being the keynote speaker, saying that her theme will be "Love Will Keep Us Together." Virginia assured Cheryl that Carlene would love to speak for this event. Virginia mentioned Carlene as a guest speaker on her radio talk show and the complement Carlene received from the manager.

Meanwhile in Baghdad, Iraq, Kirk went to his commander offices to request leave to attend the family in Georgia.

"Good morning, sir. I hope I'm not catching you at a bad time, but I have a problem and I believe you can provide assistance," Kirk said.

"Sergeant, what is your problem?

"Well, sir, I want to request leave to attend my family's reunion in Macon, Georgia. I know this is short notice, but the mission task had been completed. All security tasks have been assigned and monitors are on guards. I even assigned someone to perform my duties during my absence."

"Well, Sergeant, how can I deny you emergency leave?

That is what you are requesting, Sergeant, an emergency leave. I cannot deny you that, so you have my approval for ten days emergency leave."

Kirk saluted the commander and gave him a hand shake. "Thank you, sir."

"Now that's an outstanding Marine."

The Slaughters arrived in Macon, Georgia, for the family reunion held at the Crown Hotel. The day of the Banquet, family and friends arrived. Mrs. Slaughter and her sister were busy decorating the banquet room. At Mrs. Slaughter's home, Carlos and his family were there mingling with family. The phone rang and Kesha answered then gave it to Virginia, saying the person wanted to speak to uncle Carlos, who just left in the car. Virginia answered the phone, and it was Kirk. Kirk had arrived in Macon and was at the hotel but needed to come by grandma Slaughter's house to change clothes. He wanted his arrival to be a surprise for his mother Shelia and grandma Slaughter. Virginia pretended Kirk was one of Carlos's friends and told Kirk that she will get back with him once she tracks down Carlos. Minutes later, Carlos returned, Virginia filled him in on the surprise and they secretly departed the house with Carlene joining them. They arrived at the Crown and Virginia entered the hotel to track down Kirk. Mrs. Slaughter sister pulled Virginia to the side as she entered the lobby informing her that Kirk had arrived. Virginia informed them that she knows and she is here to pick him up. Kirk entered the hotel and hugged Virginia, saying that he saw Carlos in front of building and told him what he wanted him to do.

The moment had arrived for the family, friends, and guests to gather in the banquet room. Cheryl was at the head table with the guest speakers. She immediately began the program with the appearance of a special guest who traveled many miles to be a part of this event.

She requested that Shelia joined her to greet our special guest for this event. The room became silent, the entrance doors slowly opened and Kirk was dressed in a black suit walking slowly like a stallion down the isles to greet his mother. This cheerful moment was not only for Shelia, but for all family and friends to were among them once again. Shelia, in tears, hugged her son, and grandma Slaughter walked toward the head table to greet her beloved grandson. Her dream of joy and faith had been answered. This was just the beginning of the highlights of events. Next was Kesha's introduction of Carlene as the keynote guest speaker. This was the night of Carlene's debut. Carlene's speech penetrated the audience as she revealed her expression of the structure of a strong family foundation. Carlene's speech was based on the structure and foundation of a family presenting the challenges of her childhood life and family lifestyle. Her speech revealed the emptiness she experienced of limited time spent with grandma Slaughter due to her father's chosen career in the military. Carlene quoted, "I can recall the time I would chat with my grandma in the kitchen as she prepared the food on the table." Her parents' support and love, her brother's motto of success, "It's not what you know, it's who you know is the key to success." Her father's favorite quote, "Use your brains and think, it don't hurt." The rooms in her family home expressing the strong foundation of what they represented, her mother's independence, strength and phenomenal educational talent a symbol of the Hope Diamond the anchor of her family success and the twenty-nine years of marriage, she desired to have someday with the one she loved. This was Carlene's message of love keeping families together, sharing a powerful deliverance among friends and family. After the event, Virginia, Tricia, Carlos, and family and friends bestowed lovely compliments about Carlene's speech. For those family and friends who may have questions about how this family survived with great success Carlene mend their questionable hearts forever, for the Slaughters is a family that is not afraid to open their doors to many challenges, because they are a family of strong faith as individual, team, and family unity.

*****

It is time to bring this story of a young couple, native of Macon, Georgia, who did not have any idealism they wanted to achieve, but through the roaring, challenging journey throughout the military communities, they learned to except and adapt, adjust with flexibility to achieve their destiny with success.

To those who read this story of great courage and faith we embraced you to enter the legacy of *Vision of Change*, the sequel novel of *Til Death Do Us Part: Marriage Survives the Stress of Military Life*, a life that's will inspire and bring change to all your endeavors.

The end.

ADDITIONAL BOOKS BY
VIRANDA I. SLAPPY

Til Death Do Us Part: A Marriage
Survives the Stress of Military Life

The summer of 1975 revealed the relationship of two black teenagers, Virginia Cottingham and Carlos Slaughter who went from friends to lovers to married couples. Virginia's ex-lover Teddy, returned to town with intentions to recapture his relationship with her, but found she was engaged to be married to Slaughter. Teddy, furious with this news, confronted Slaughter. Slaughter and Virginia's relationship went on shaky ground when Virginia suspected Slaughter cheating on her. Virginia confirmed her pregnancy, and Slaughter joins the army.

Slaughter got drunk and had a one-night-stand with Judy. The marital infidelity unfolds. Virginia gave birth, and Slaughter discovers that Larry, one of their friends, had feelings for Virginia and took his family to his first duty station in Fort Campbell, Kentucky.

Slaughter has been contacted to testify in a former drill sergeant's trial. Virginia discovers Judy's letters. Virginia confronts Slaughter about Judy. Slaughter threatens to shoot Iris, his neighbor. Slaughter is assigned to Germany. Priscilla and Hillary (Virginia's girlfriends), battle over Priscilla's involvement with Hillary's husband, and Mrs. Connors' husband finds her with another soldier. Slaughter discovers Virginia's exposure to drugs and alcohol.

AUTHOR'S NOTES

Regulatory guidance for the Married Army Couples Program (MACP) can be found in AR 614-200 (Enlisted Assignments and Utilization Management), AR 614-30 (Overseas Service), and AR 614-100 (Officer Assignment Policies, Details, and Transfers).

Married, regular army couples desiring assignments to establish a common household may request enrollment in the MACP. When one member of the couple is not an active army soldier, they may not enroll in the program but may request reassignment to join their spouse if they are married to a member of another U.S. military service or to a member of the reserve components who is called to active duty for one year or more.

Married army couples must be enrolled on the HQDA Total Army Personnel Data Base (TAPDB) to be considered for joint assignment. Under the MACP, both soldiers will be considered for a joint assignment at the point when either of the two is nominated by Total Officer Personnel Management System (TOPMIS) or the Enlisted Distribution Assignment System (EDAS). If the assignment is from continental U.S. to overseas, PERSCOM will coordinate the two requirements with the appropriate overseas command or liaison office. Both soldiers will receive their assignments/pinpoint assignments in the same TOPMIS/EDAS cycle, or the special instructions in the assignment instructions will state that a married Army couple assignment was considered but could not be accommodated.

Enrollment is a simple process of verifying that two soldiers are married to one another and having this information transmitted from the servicing military personnel division/personnel service battalion to the TAPDB. A separate standard installation/division personnel system transaction is required for each spouses' social security number and component (i.e., commissioned, warrant, or enlisted) to be entered on the master files of both soldiers. Once enrolled, both soldiers will be continuously considered for joint assignments. Enrollment in the MACP guarantees that both soldiers will be considered for a joint assignment. Although readiness is the number one priority, the Enlisted Personnel Management Directorate strives to accommodate joint domiciles whenever possible.

Another great tool of information housing is attending your Army Community Service. They provide information about the gaining installation community. Are you a member of the active duty reservists employed with Department of Defense Civilian Service with questions about restoring benefits entitlements (Federal Employees Health Benefit (FEHB) or Federal Employees Group Life, Thrift Savings) and submitting your retirement package? As an employee you need to visit Army Benefit Center website: www.abc.army.mil or your local Civilian Personnel Advisory Center for assistance. For information about Office Personnel Management (OPM) procedures in processing or how to apply for retirement visit the www.opm.gov/retire.

For those active duty members who are discontinuing their enlistment with active duty injuries, you need to ensure that all medical documentation of illness/injuries are continuous treatment are in your active duty medical records, make copies of medical records for your personnel usage when filing for Veteran Disability. During your out processing terminal leave or prior to out processing terminal leave enlistment visit your local Veteran Administration for information on how to file your claim and remember to always get a second Civilian physician's diagnosis of illness and appeal whatever percentage Veteran Administration Hospital evaluation of your injury while on active duty to increase your medical or retirement annuity for fair compensation.

Viranda I. Slappy

Website: www.virandaslappyauthor.com
Twitter: https://twitter.com/virandaslappy
Facebook: https://www.facebook.com/viranda.slappy

Biography

Viranda Irene Nottingham-Slappy, born June 27, 1957 in Macon, Georgia. She is the daughter of the late Willie James Nottingham, Sr. and Viriam Purnell Bowman. She is a graduate of Northeast High School and Los Angeles Community College. She has Associate Degree, General Studies in Business Management graduate of Central Texas College, Fort Riley, Kansas. Employment is with Department of Defense, United States Army Civil Service. Employment histories at Fort Riley, Kansas are Irwin Community Army Community Hospital, 1st Personnel Service Battalion and present employer Army Benefit Center-Civilian.

Viranda is a woman of many talents. She has received many awards for recognition of her outstanding performances. Her acknowledged awards are an Achievement Medal for Civilian Service, Officially Commended for Exemplary Performance, Sustained Superior Performance, Certificate of Achievement for Exceptional

Performance and Community Organizational Outstanding Distinguished Services.

She is the wife of John Cecil Slappy, Sr. (29 years of marriage), retired soldier from the United States Army and Department of Defense Civil Service employee at Fort Riley, Kansas. Mother of two children and one grandson, Zsashamica Demetricus Slappy, graduate of Fort Hays State University, Bachelor of Arts and Master of Science, employee of University of Kansas, located in Lawrence, Kansas, John Cecil Slappy, Jr., employee of Citi-Span, Overland Park, Kansas and the proud grandmother of Gevon John Kimbrel Slappy. She is the sibling of Willie James Nottingham, Jr., Patricia Ann Fennelle, Michael Allen Nottingham and the granddaughter of Willie Mae Purnell and the late Thomas J. Purnell, all residence of Macon, Georgia.

In her leisure time, author of books, *Til Death Do Us Part: A Marriage Survives the Stress of Military Life* and *Generation Impact: An American Family's Turmoil*. She is a member, Past Matron of St. Tabitha, Order of Eastern Stars, member of Heriones of Jericho, 1st Lt. Daughter of Isis, Cyrenes of Prince Hall of Affiliation, Free and Accepted Masonry of Kansas Jurisdiction, former host and producer of Express Yourself radio talk show, NAACP, reporter-writer for *Uplifter Newsletter*, Second Missionary Baptist Church and Adjutant General Corps Regimental Association, Bison Chapter, Fort Riley, Kansas.